CW00553860

GIFTED

GIFTED

SUZUMI SUZUKI

translated by allison markin powell

SCRIBE

Melbourne | London | Minneapolis

Scribe Publications
18–20 Edward St, Brunswick, Victoria 3056, Australia
2 John St, Clerkenwell, London, WC1N 2ES, United Kingdom
3754 Pleasant Ave, Suite 100, Minneapolis, Minnesota 55409, USA

First published in Japanese by Bungeishunju Ltd. in 2022
Published in English by Scribe 2024
English-language translation rights reserved throughout the United
Kingdom and Commonwealth except Canada by Scribe Publications
Pty Ltd under the license granted by Suzumi Suzuki, arranged with
Bungeishunju Ltd. through The English Agency (Japan) Ltd. and
New River Literary Ltd.

Copyright © Suzumi Suzuki 2022
Translation copyright © Allison Markin Powell 2024

All rights reserved. Without limiting the rights under copyright
reserved above, no part of this publication may be reproduced,
stored in or introduced into a retrieval system, or transmitted, in
any form or by any means (electronic, mechanical, photocopying,
recording or otherwise) without the prior written permission
of the publishers of this book.

The moral rights of the author and translator have been asserted.

Internal pages designed by Transit Books

Printed and bound in the UK by CPI Group (UK) Ltd, Croydon
CR0 4YY

Scribe is committed to the sustainable use of natural resources and
the use of paper products made responsibly from those resources.

978 1 761380 44 0 (Australian edition)
978 1 915590 78 7 (UK edition)
978 1 761386 08 4 (ebook)

Catalogue records for this book are available from the
National Library of Australia and the British Library.

scribepublications.com.au
scribepublications.co.uk
scribepublications.com

GIFTED

I go around the back of the building that faces the road separating Koreatown and the entertainment district, push open the heavy door at the rear of the car park, and ascend the interior staircase. On the third floor, I heave my weight against another heavy door that leads to a hallway, and once it opens wide enough there is always a metallic creak. While that door slowly closes, I put the key in the lock for the door to my own apartment, turn it to the left, and hear a click as the latch releases. These are the two sounds I hear every night when I come home. If the interval between the creaking of the hinges and the turning of the pins in the old lock cylinder is too long or too short, there will be no sense of security. If I'm carrying something heavy and have to set it on the floor or if I carelessly drop my keys, the rhythm breaks.

Perhaps because there had been too much lost over the summer, in the days before autumn fully set in, I readily agreed to my mother's request to move into my apartment. The illness dwelling within her stomach had finally progressed to the stage where her basic survival was untenable, and it seemed she was looking for a place to die.

Just one more poem, I want to finish writing just one more, my mother said over the phone.

"I can't do it from a hospital bed. You understand, don't you?"

Though I detected a sense of entitlement embedded in that "You understand, don't you?" it no longer angered or irritated me. I even felt sorry for her—that as death approached, she would regard my apartment on the fringes of the entertainment district as more desirable than an ordinary hospital room. In the end, my mother had not enjoyed the lofty success she hoped for. She had published several slender volumes of poetry, her lovely face had been featured alongside various magazine interviews, and she had once appeared on a local station's morning program to read an English poet's work in Japanese. That was it.

My mother moved from the hospital to my place two days after that phone call. My feelings were evenly split between wishing she had given me more notice so that I could have taken care of my own business and been better prepared, and a sense of relief that my mother was convinced I wouldn't reject her as an interloper in my home. Arriving in a taxi, my mother wore baggy slacks and a long-sleeved T-shirt with a jacket she'd managed to hang over her shoulders. She must have been wearing that navy-blue jacket on the day she was admitted to the hospital—now that she was already living in loose-fitting pajamas, it was the only vestige of her former lifestyle. She had brought just two bags to the hospital, and when I offered to go to her place to get anything else she might need, she said it wasn't necessary. One of the bags was packed with two sets of pajamas, a toothbrush, and a comb, and as for my mother's other bag, which I recognized—I knew what its contents were without even having to look inside.

It had been almost eight years since my mother and I slept in the same room—since about the time when terrorists crashed those airplanes into the Twin Towers in New York—and with the exception of the last two or three years of my teens, it's not as if we'd been out of touch. After I realized how unexpectedly grave my mother's illness was, we were in quite frequent contact—I had even met up with her and visited her at the hospital. Still, it had been a while since I'd seen her, and I was anxious about how frail she was likely to be, how thin her hair would have become. When she was younger, her lustrous, jet-black tresses had been long enough to cover her breasts. In contrast to my own frizzy brownish hair, hers was too thick for a perm or even to tie back, she said, insisting on keeping it straight and wearing it down, even in summer. When her bangs got too unruly to be brushed back, she would go to a salon—not the one I went to in our neighborhood, of course—and come home with hair that was shinier than ever.

Although in the spring of last year my mother had declared her intention to survive, she no longer seemed to have the same resolve. As it turned out, she stayed at my apartment for a mere nine days—never even opening her work bag to take out a pen—before she developed difficulty breathing and had to return to the hospital. Had we had half a year together, or even just a few months, each day I could have made food she might have been able to enjoy, could have given her relaxing baths, could have talked to her about things she might have found interesting, even if she hadn't listened to most of what I said . . . Thinking back now, at least, I feel like, after getting her to take her medications and putting her to bed, keeping to the same schedule as at the hospital, I shouldn't have left her alone. The only time we both slept there together was on the night she arrived. My mother may have thought I had been granted just two days off, but the truth was, work only took up a fraction of the time I was out.

I could tell that, once my mother sensed I was about to go out for the night, she was trying to get me to stay—she would deliberately dawdle with her meds, or spread open the newspaper, straining to come up with questions to ask. *Don't go, stay here, let's be together*—she never said anything like that. Instead, she would show me the TV and radio listings in the paper, pressing buttons on the remote control and wondering aloud, "Is there something distracting to watch before bed?" My mother's arms, slender and supple when she was healthy, had grown much hairier and were now thinner than the span of my first three fingers. Her skin was so dry and ashy that I bought some inexpensive moisturizing cream at the drugstore and rubbed it in for her, which brought back some of her color, and again she said, "Let's look for something interesting to watch together." Though I rarely watched TV, her desperate attempts to engage in idle conversation put me even more on edge. *Get me the hell out of here*, I'd think to myself.

I'd wait until the very last minute to change my clothes, and even then, I avoided putting on outfits that looked like I was heading to the entertainment district. Whereas normally I'd take an hour to put on makeup and powder my skin, I started doing all that once I was already out. And somehow, the simple and modest guises I put on to keep my mother from stalling me seemed to her liking. There was one time when she said, "You look pretty today." I was wearing a beige cardigan over jeans. It was the first time my mother had ever complimented my clothing or appearance. But I still ended up going out every night, after the meds had been administered and the questions had been dodged. When I left her as she dropped off to sleep, I hated the sound of the key as I locked the door from the outside.

Had my mother been more straightforwardly conceited or more self-aggrandizing, she might have had an easier time of it. Though not tall, she had high hips, a strong nose, and big broad eyes. Her delicately pale skin would burn under the hot summer sun, so she avoided going to the beach or the pool. She knew very well that being beautiful was something she had been blessed with, yet she scorned those who spoke of women as "great beauties" or made similar comments about their appearance. Such was her nature, and it manifested with her creative work—she never seemed to get the compliments she originally hoped for from a certain kind of people who praised her poems. I suppose it's inevitable that such a complicated sense of self-respect would be construed as prickliness, at least superficially. She would get close to people for a short time, but after a while, there would be no further mention or sight of them. As I recall the ones my mother considered friends, it's years now since I've heard any of their names. The fact that, seen from the outside, the life my mother lived hadn't seemed terribly lonely or unhappy may have been largely due to the grace of her physical appearance. All the more reason why I had tried not to look at her gaunt and fuzzy limbs or her thinning hair.

On the ninth day, I made my mother noodles in warm broth garnished with kujo scallions and mentaiko. I had been out until the morning and I was sleepy, but having grown impatient with my mother never answering when I asked what she might be able to eat, I'd gone ahead and made this, using up leftover somen I bought at the beginning of the summer. I usually keep ingredients on hand for making somen and hot pot, but the kujo scallions and mentaiko were items I bought specifically when my mother came to stay. She took a mouthful from the small red bowl set on the low table I had put beside the futon quilt and said it was delicious. She brought the food to her lips three or four times, then set down her chopsticks. There had only been a few noodles in the bowl, yet you could barely tell she had eaten any.

"Such a delicious meal, but I can't eat another bite!"

As she sits there on the bedding, looking apologetic from across the cheap table I bought at a mass-market store, her words don't seem in keeping with her appearance in these, her final days. Beneath the soft material of her long-sleeved, worn-in pajamas, she doesn't even have on underwear. These must be from the shop at the hospital. Being sick, she wouldn't have the energy to shop for clothes, and it's improbable that my mother would choose yellow, floral-print pajamas for herself. More likely that a visiting acquaintance had been pressed into service, even if I hardly ever saw anyone come by her hospital room. I was reminded of several of the images that often stood for death and funerals in her poems, and felt a pit in my own stomach.

"It's fine, doesn't matter. Don't feel like you have to eat it."

It isn't my intention to sound indifferent, but my words reverberate with an unnecessary chill. The light that shines through the yellowed lace curtains looks like it would set the carpet aflame, as if it were summer. I can't bear to sit there on my dingy cushion, so I put down the larger bowl with my portion in it and hurriedly stand up to clear my mother's dish, heading toward the sink in that same room. There are only two rooms, and one of them is crammed with a bed and my clothes and purses—I opted not to put my mother in there. Instead, I wanted to conduct all aspects of my mother's life within the now bare and spacious room where there's a sink, the door that leads to the bath, and the door to the toilet. I know that, in her current state, my mother doesn't have the strength to criticize my designer purses or dresses for being tacky, but I still don't want her to see them.

"I'm sorry," my mother said. My delivery indeed must have come off as either angry or cold or exasperated. It's strange for my mother to apologize for not being able to eat more. And yet, I wanted her to apologize to me—it didn't matter what for. Not wanting her to see my face, I got rid of my mother's uneaten noodles at the sink, and as I was washing her bowl, I became aware of her approaching me with slow, tottering steps. Even as I sensed this, I remained unconvinced by the figure reflected in the frosted-glass window facing the sink. Going to the toilet was the only thing my mother could just manage to do by herself—for brushing her teeth and washing her face, I would bring over a washbasin and water so she could do these things while sitting on the futon.

She came up right behind me, saying "I'm sorry" again, and rubbed the back of my arm over my tattoo. Without turning around, I kept scrubbing the bowl much longer than was required. Before my mother came here, I seldom ever used the sponge, so it had been practically brand new, but after one week's time it had yellowed, and one side of it was frayed. The area where I live is noisy at night, but during the daytime, you hardly hear any voices at all. People come and go in Koreatown across the big road, but even in summer, this side of the street doesn't come alive until after the sun goes down, once it's completely dark. You always hear engines roaring by, eventually seeming to fade into the distance. The area around my tattoo ached under my mother's touch.

Wearing those floral-print pajamas, my mother came right up behind me until she was virtually touching my back. "I feel like there's more I could have taught you," she said. She was so preternaturally thin that, were I to move my hand or arm, I might have knocked her right over. I put down the yellow sponge, my left hand still gripping the sudsy bowl for a moment. The water dribbling out of the faucet made an unpleasant sound as it struck the old silver sink.

"I ran out of time. Really and truly. Even though I feel like there's so much I need to teach you."

I made a noise out of my nose as if in response and remained still for a few seconds, but then, slowly, I moved my hand to run the bowl under the faucet and rinse off the dish soap. It had been more than twenty-five years since I'd tumbled out of my mother's womb, seventeen of which we had spent under the same roof, so my mother's complaint, issued from within those yellow, floral-print pajamas—that there were things left to tell me but she just hadn't been given enough time—set me even further on edge. To be sure, though, until I had assumed full control over my body, my mother probably hadn't felt the need to explain anything to me. My mother had never been married. And even after birthing me out of her own skin, my body had been hers and hers alone, at least until I was able to feed myself.

Perhaps standing up had tired her, because at some point I became aware of her slowly making her way back toward the futon, and at last, I turned to face her. The still-oppressive sunlight pierced the dingy lace curtains and fell upon the bedding I had laid out in the middle of the room, thinking it would be convenient for getting to the toilet and eating meals. I waited as she walked, unsteady on her feet, in those tacky pajamas. With my mother, I always felt like an outsider. Even though the kitchen was part of the same room that faced the exterior corridor, with only the frosted-glass window, it was dim during the daytime unless you turned on the light. I watched my mother's back, so frail that even in the shadows I could see her spine through the pajamas.

My upper arm where she had touched me was still warm. Under the tattoo, the skin was discolored, red and white, the scar from a burn. The woman walking feebly across the room in my apartment, more than half of her once-beautiful hair now gone, she is the one who burned me.

That same evening I took my mother, unable to breathe and panicked, to the hospital in a taxi. For the two weeks since then, I've been visiting her there around the same time every day. Family members who register in advance are permitted to come and go in the middle of the night or early in the morning, which means that every night I could theoretically stay by my mother's side until she drifts off to sleep. But often I don't feel like going straight home from the hospital, so I end up spending the morning and midday there, and at some point in the afternoon I leave. After killing time in my neighborhood, if I feel like it, then I go to work at the bar. With the sound of the key in the latch still ringing in my ears, I use my weight to push the door inward, and as I reenter the apartment I live in alone, my eye catches sight of, there directly on the low table, the leftover crust of bread I'd eaten in a rush before going out that morning. I've no memory of leaving it there, but there's no other possibility—it had to have been me. Now that two weeks have passed, there are no more left-behind items or strands of hair to be found, no longer any trace to signal that someone other than myself had been sleeping here. For the first three days, I had left the futon bedding spread out beside the table, assuming my mother would be back after receiving treatment. But by the third day, it became clear that she wouldn't return. I threw the sheets into the washing machine, put the futon quilt in its plastic storage bag, and moved the table back where it belonged. When I moved in and set up this apartment, I bought a basic bedding set for when a friend might stay over, and that's what I had put out for my mother to sleep on. It'd been used maybe three times by one friend or another, but I hadn't taken it out of the bag in almost two years.

I toss the bread crust into the covered trash can on the edge of the kitchen, take off my denim jacket and put it on a hanger, then go into the bathroom to wash my hands. The container of hand soap with an illustration of a typical family on it is almost empty—I noticed this several days ago but have again forgotten to buy more. I don't feel like going out to the twenty-four-hour drugstore just to get hand soap. I know I'll be at the hospital tomorrow until the afternoon, and I figure if I work the pump, I can squeeze out enough liquid for at least one or two more handwashings. Compared to the hospital or the neighborhood outside, my apartment has such a sense of reality that once I come home, I don't want to go back out. I wet my hands and am surprised, when I push down on the pump, by the amount of actual soap—rather than mostly air—that comes out, so I wash my hands diligently, drying them on the bath towel I used after that morning's shower, and then sit down in front of the low table where my mother's bedding had been. I briefly consider taking a sleeping pill, but decide against it—whether because I am about to get my period, or from lack of sleep, or from the shochu I can still feel the effects of, I figure I'll be able to fall asleep.

Since last week I've left a paper catch-all box that I got as a prize for my leftover pachinko balls on the table. I'd replaced the empty can that I'd been using as an ashtray, so the tabletop looked a bit different than it had over the summer. While my mother was here, I had tried my best to go outside to smoke—or at the very least, to only smoke under the fan. Thinking this would be a good excuse to quit smoking, I had gotten rid of all my ashtrays on the first day of her stay, but it wasn't even three hours later that all I could think about was cigarettes. My mother seemed to have quit smoking before her illness was detected, but now that I think about it, I don't remember exactly when. I pulled the ashtray toward me, switched on the TV for background noise, and put on socks. This is an old building, and my apartment gets cold. Up until two weeks ago, the sunshine had felt like summer, but now, once the sun sets, the floor doesn't retain even a hint of its warmth. I could hear the voice of a familiar entertainer on the TV—there was something pleasant about his exaggerated, suggestive exuberance, so I left that channel on and lay down atop the pile of laundry on the carpet. I want to turn on the heater, but even with the cord stretched as far as it will go, it still doesn't reach over by the table, so I'd have to get up and take a few steps toward the kitchen. Having taken off my jacket and now wearing only a light layer, I have no choice but to reach into the bed of laundry and pull out something warm to wrap myself up in. My throat hurts from smoking too many cigarettes at the bar, but regardless, still lying there, I pull out the pack in my back pocket and put another one in my mouth—though I seem to have left my lighter somewhere. I look in the leather purse I carried around all day but no luck.

I try to recall what I've eaten since leaving the house that day, but I don't remember anything other than the coffee I bought at the stand right across the way on the big road. When I drink alcohol, I can't remember things from before I was drunk. Then, when I sober up, I can't remember things from when I was drunk. This is not a recent thing—it's been this way for a long time, ever since I left home at seventeen and drinking became part of my work. What remains is only a vague recollection of half the day, and I spend the other half making memories that will soon vanish. Whether delusions or hallucinations, hazy, dreamlike memories do sometimes rear their heads, and I'm always a bit disappointed when things I only wish were illusions turn out to be all too real. But actually my recollection from around one in the morning—of ordering Chinese food at the karaoke bar with terrible acoustics that an acquaintance ten years older than me opened on the edge of the entertainment district, someone I knew from the place where I quit hostessing last year—probably did happen. I must have ordered bitter melon stir-fry, which is the only item worth eating from the delivery service you get at all those cabaret clubs or love hotels.

I may be better off just sleeping here like this. The lace curtains double-hung over the blackout drapes haven't been opened in days, my cell phone is plugged in on the table, and I don't have the energy to move to the room that's even chillier, where the only bed is. I slept on the same pile of laundry yesterday too. On the table is a paperback, an incomprehensible detective novel by an American author—I only read the translator's afterword, and the bookmark has been sticking out from the same place for quite a while. I pull the book down onto the floor, open it to where the bookmark is, and see the words "alcohol-induced delirium," which only intensify my drowsiness. My cell glows for an instant, and the cheap table makes a strange noise as the phone vibrates for less than a second. I hold the phone at an angle so I can see it from my prone position—there's a notification, a message from a friend. I have a bad feeling, and when I raise my head, I have the unpleasant sensation that I am about to regurgitate the contents of my stomach.

I yank on the cell phone's charging cord to pull it down and open the message. The word *funeral* leaps rudely before my eyes, but this has nothing to do with the burial rites for my dying mother. It's about a miserable ceremony that took place in the scorching heat.

I lost two friends over the summer. One was a friend from junior high who, despite having a kid more than five years ago and being married, had run off with a man and disappeared. Previously, though, she had kept in touch with me consistently, even though I only ever hung out with people from around here. If this neighborhood or my apartment had seemed like an escape for her, then our connection struck me as rather tenuous. That's how I'd felt since she'd been gone, anyway. We used to text pretty regularly but didn't meet up in person very often—for every three times she suggested it, we'd get together once for a proper lunch. That was the level of our friendship. *I've met someone*, she had told me cheerfully in a stream of texts. She had seemed to approach these dates with the light-hearted restraint of a married woman. *Guess that's how it goes*, I had thought, and when she had gradually grown heartsick about it, and started visiting a fortune teller in Ebisu, I had thought, *Guess that's also how it goes*. Her affair, the fortune-telling, running off with her lover—I have no idea how run-of-the-mill it all is, or if it's unusual. But

23

one day, there were no more text replies, and after a while, my messages weren't even going through. I got a call from her husband, whom I had only met once. He told me that she had always been erratic about what time she would come home, but one day, she just never returned. The child was still living with him. He asked me where she could have gone, but I had no idea either.

The other friend had jumped to her death from a rental condo in Osaka. I had seen her dead body laid out at the funeral, so at least I knew where she had gone.

She had been the kind of person who would say, at various times, that she wanted to die, and among our friends, we tended to take this to mean that, interchangeably, she was in a bad mood, or something sad had happened, or she was feeling lonely. Ever since we met, about three years ago when one of my customers brought her to the bar where I worked for a drink, she had seemed like she didn't much like being alive.

"This is Eri. Her name is one letter different from yours."

That was how the customer had introduced her to me. He went on, "But I doubt those are your real names." He laughed, but both she and I were working under our real names. This customer had a tacky habit of hosting dinner gatherings, bringing together women to whom he'd taken a fancy. Naturally, all of them were having sex with him for money, so often one of the five or six women present would throw herself at him, to try to prove to the others that they didn't all have the same standing. Though it was a mystery whom she was trying to prove it to—probably to herself, I guess. But the real pity is, when it comes to women like that, there isn't a whit of difference among us, we're all in the same position. In this world, there are people who matter and people who don't, and what that group of us all had in common was that, as far as the world was concerned, none of us mattered much. The woman who died seemed unbothered by such a notion, and in that regard, she and I and another one of the women had clicked, managing to keep in touch even after we'd kicked that guy to the curb.

The message on my phone is from that third friend. She makes a killing turning tricks at a high-end place in a district packed with bathhouses. Her face is pretty enough—she has dark hair, fair skin, no scars or tattoos—and you had to have at least a D-cup to work there.

—I mentioned these places at the funeral, forgot about it but sending them both now. First one is where Eri used to work, it's a big place, but also gets a bad rap because it's big. Seems like it has three different rankings. Second one has high-quality clientele and girls, but no way to know how much business actually comes in.

The funeral had been in Eri's hometown, the location not very easy for city dwellers to get to. After a rather long train ride, you had to take a bus—there weren't any taxis at the train station. It was probably the first time I'd been on a bus since my elementary-school field trips. The only consolation was that you could use the same transit card for the train and the bus—but everything else about that journey had been a real drag. Maybe that was why, on the way back, I had feigned interest in S&M bars to this friend. I had mostly forgotten about it, as, it seemed, had she, up until right now. With the dispassionate manner of a woman who worked at a high-end bathhouse, she had sent two links at the end of her pithy summaries.

—I'll take a good look at these later. Wonder what ranking Eri was?

With my cell phone still attached to its charger, I held the device directly above my face, using one hand to send off a reply. *I should have thanked her first*, I thought, just as I hit the send button, but the screen showed that it had already gone through. Shows how ungrateful I am.

I feel a dull ache in my upper arm from holding up my phone. At bars, too, the pay varies wildly from one person to another, but except for your first few months, your hourly rate is calculated by how much you sell and how often you work. I have no idea what determines rankings at a place where you have to get naked. As I contemplated what Eri's going rate might have been, I touched the outer part of my arm where it ached. There are two lilies and one snake that extend onto my back, in order to fully cover my burn scars. Whenever anyone asks me why lilies, the only reason I offer is that peonies are associated with the yakuza. When I was a kid, my mother only ever bought cut flowers if they were on sale, and she had a few potted plants she would water, but I don't remember her setting out lilies.

I rouse myself, setting my phone on the table, and walk toward the kitchen, where, behind the sink, on the sill of the frosted-glass window, there are several lighters, and I use one of them to light my cigarette. I've had it in my mouth since before, when I was looking for a lighter, so the tip is moist. Even though it's my own saliva, once it's outside of my own body, I find it dirty and gross. I open the refrigerator aimlessly, and as I'm staring inside at the assortment of half-finished cans of booze, my phone makes a sound on the table, so I go back over to it without taking anything out of the fridge.

—Dunno about this place's facial standards, but maybe not a very high rank? Not just b/c of her scars, she was on the bony side, and she had teeth implants and a dark side. Tho for S&M, some guys look for low-ranking girls, not just for financial reasons.

—Right, forgot about her teeth. But I've heard a lot of S&M clients are doctors and lawyers. Those types have money.

As we send messages back and forth, it occurs to me to wonder what happens to dental implants when you're cremated. For that matter, I don't know if your original teeth burn up either.

Sometimes, when the three of us got together, we would go straight to a friend's bar and drink there until four thirty in the morning. Eri didn't have a particularly low tolerance for alcohol, but one time—maybe she hadn't been feeling well or just drank too much—she ended up in the toilet, puking her guts out. The toilet was right behind the seats at the counter of the small bar; she'd been in there for a while, and we could hear it all—retching, vomit hitting the bowl, water running.

None of us were especially worried, but once it seemed like she might have been feeling better, we heard her voice from inside say, "Sorry, could you . . . ?" Someone shouted, "What's the matter?" and the door opened. "I fell down," Eri said, splayed out on the floor, and there was a gaping hole where what clearly should have been there in her mouth wasn't. Her upper front teeth—all four of them, maybe even more—were completely gone.

Around here, there were plenty of people missing things that should have been there, and yet this was such an unexpected sight that all of us at the bar, including the owner, were hysterical with laughter, the tension broken in the wee hours of the morning. Ultimately, I think it was the guy who owned the bar that came to the rescue, using a set of wooden chopsticks to retrieve her teeth.

At the time, Eri had been working four days a week as an on-call dominatrix in the city, and she was relatively cheerful about it. She had a small dog and was living on her own, not too far from my place, on a street that was sort of near the gay area. I had gone over there to hang out with the friend from the bathhouse. The apartment was cramped and cluttered, and smelled a bit doggy. I had been the last to arrive after getting off work at the bar. All I managed to bring were a few cans of Hyoketsu shochu and Tanrei beer and some water I'd picked up at a convenience store in Shinjuku Ni-chome. The woman from the bathhouse had already started drinking, and though she had brought some dried snacks and cheap shochu too, we still ended up going out on two more booze runs. The second time, I stood on the street smoking a cigarette before going into the convenience store, and the sky was already getting light.

That's right, Eri didn't smoke, I recall. That's why I only hung out at her place the one time. I had been to the apartment where the woman from the bathhouse lived with a guy many times. That place was on the east side of the entertainment district, a spacious condo where you could smoke inside. She lives there on her own now.

—What happened to the dog that was at Eri's place?

I ask this even though I don't have much interest in the small dog—I'm on my second cigarette, not knowing when the exchange will end.

—She'd been working away from home, so I doubt the dog's still at her place. Might be at a friend's?

—A friend who would look after the dog for her? The dog's not dead? Maybe the dog died and then she started working away from home, the gig with guaranteed pay?

—Now I remember. That host guy has her dog.

Eri was a year older than me and had been living and working around these streets since she was a teenager, when she'd left her hometown with its horrible traffic. About a year ago, she'd stopped working at the bars in the city and started doing ten-day or two-week temp gigs with guaranteed day rates. At first she would get in touch whenever she was back in town, but at some point I stopped hearing from her. On rare occasions, there'd be a text from wherever she was, saying she wanted to die, or she was going to die, but we were pretty inured to it. After going out to Osaka for a gig, apparently she started working as a regular for a delivery-health call service there that she seemed to like, and for those last two months, she had been renting a place by the week. She hadn't moved out of her place here, so she was making enough to cover rent for both apartments.

I knew the host, whom Eri had referred to as a consultant. I doubt they were sexually involved—Eri had said herself that she wasn't really attracted to him. She would go see him regularly at his club, and as far as I could tell, it was a sensible routine—someone who would listen to her complaints for the price of a few drinks, even with the table charge and shimei fee. It was pretty tame, and any girl around here has done the same kind of thing at least once.

—She didn't drop all that much money on the guy. I wonder why she switched to working away gigs? She was in better shape when she was here.

—She was throwing money at someone else too. It wasn't always the same person. She'd get hooked on someone, then after a while, there'd be a new guy. But I don't know why she started doing away gigs. Maybe she stopped getting customers where she was working, or some creep was hanging around her here. Though I hear lately a lot more girls are picking up those kinds of gigs, so she might have just been scouted?

—Had she been here, tho, we might have stopped her when she sent a message about wanting to die.

—Come on, there's no way we could've known. Whenever she sent those texts before, I'd call her up and ask her out for a drink, but I never took her seriously. Cuz she herself didn't mean it seriously. I know tons of people, both customers and women, who say they want to die. But only a small percentage—even less, it's more like the odds of winning the lottery—actually go thru with it, so there's no way to know. Plus, when she sent those texts, I could never tell if she meant it or not.

No matter how many times I timidly brought up this subject, the woman from the bathhouse always responded with the same long and finely honed phrases. But this was our first exchange specifically about the texts Eri sent on the day she died. Despite my wondering, I truly believe there wasn't anything more I could have done. Eri didn't want to go on living, and finding reasons why she should have was beyond me.

From outside the mostly closed curtains, a patch of the dark sky is illuminated by a flashing red light—either a patrol car or an ambulance or lights from a helicopter. Not an unusual occurrence around here.

The next day, and the day after that, and the first day of the following week, I listened for the sounds of the door creaking on its hinges and my key turning the lock as I returned home. To my ears, at least, the interval formed a precise rhythm. Which is why I felt unsettled the whole time I was in the drugstore and the smoke shop, having turned back around after pushing open the door to the third floor and realizing I'd forgotten to buy cigarettes and, of course, hand soap. The doctor had told me that from now on, barring extenuating circumstances, I should try to stay at the hospital by my mother's side when she was awake, so I had decided to quit the bar.

By rights, I should have given them my notice at least a month ago—I had already stopped keeping up with my clients, and more often than not, I was either late to work or a no-show—but when I did finally tell the manager, he said I had a surprisingly strong sense of decency. It was to my advantage that in this industry, employees often simply vanished. I went to the bar before it opened, and when I told the manager my mother was in the hospital, he even gave me what little money was owed to me, instead of making me wait for payday. Showing up for work meant you could get up to ten thousand yen, paid as daily wages. As I wrote my name on the slip you had to fill out for your cash, I was convinced the manager didn't believe me about my mother. It was such a clichéd excuse for missing work or being late that in this situation, it would have been better to embellish a lie with something that rings of the truth. Something like: last spring my father was diagnosed with colon cancer and had surgery, and though he had recovered, there's been a recurrence, and he's undergoing chemo, so now it's my mother who's collapsed, from caregiver fatigue. But the reality is, my mother is dying of her illness, and there's no other way to say it, there's no version of it that rings more of the truth, though thinking back on the words that came out of my mouth just a little while ago, they sounded so hollow. Whether or not he believed me, I was just grateful to get the money I had given up hope of receiving. I'd worked in this quarter for a relatively long time and had a relatively large number of clients, so my hourly rate was high enough that even after being docked for no-shows and being late, one month's pay still added up to a pretty decent amount.

A customer I know happened to stop by the bar, so I stayed for the early shift and then I cleared out my locker. I found a paper shopping bag to bring home the dresses and shoes and small clutch I kept at the bar, and I stuffed what I bought at the twenty-four-hour drugstore—hand soap, tights, energy drinks, and eyelash glue—in there too, putting the cigarettes in my handbag, and then I climbed the stairs to the third floor again. The paper shopping bag wasn't from this neighborhood, it was from an upscale florist, and my handbag was Fendi, bought for me long ago, while I was with some businessman who owned racehorses. He said he had a stomach ulcer and told me to pick out anything I wanted from Fendi for some reason—and then he stopped coming to the bar to drink. I had figured he was going to another bar in the quarter, or that he had found a new favorite hostess at a more high-class place in a different entertainment district, but I hadn't let my suspicions show.

Upon hearing the longed-for sound of the door after heaving my weight against it, I quickly put the key I'm already holding into the lock of my apartment and turn it, and once this second anticipated sound has been confirmed, I slip inside the door. The overstuffed and bulging paper shopping bag almost gets caught in the door, which I avoid by employing a swift spiral maneuver. I put the key back in the Fendi, put the Fendi in the shopping bag, which I slide further into the room with a shove, then I twist my feet out of the straps of my shoes, grab the hand soap and eyelash glue, and go to the sink. I drop the completely empty hand soap with the illustration of the family into a plastic bag by my feet, peel open the seal on the new bottle, which has a raccoon on it, turn the water on, and then work the pump a few times. The fourth pump produces a definite result, and the fifth releases a liberal quantity of foam into my hand. Since I didn't shower this morning there isn't a towel already in use, so I shake the water off my hands and toss the eyelash glue, still in its package, onto the shelf under the sink. Now that I won't be going to work at the bar, I wonder when I'll next wear false eyelashes. There are probably about five applications in the package of glue I bought.

I wanted to fill the bathtub with hot water and soak in it, but the tub hadn't been used at all since my mother left, and it was splotched with unmistakable stains—and not the kind that could be easily rubbed off. So I gave up on the bathtub, instead turning on the hand shower at full blast until it ran hot, and using it to wash my hair and body. Last week, at the start of the month, the weather had suddenly turned cold. With the hot shower beating against my back, I used cleansing oil to remove my makeup before wetting my face, then turned the front of my body toward the shower, keeping my oil-smeared face raised upward. The moment the water hit it, the oil emulsified and streamed down my face to my shoulders and upper arms, and with the help of this viscous liquid,

I peeled off the tape I use to hide my tattoo, making a cracking sound. I hate having any residue of the adhesive left on my skin, so several years ago I devised this routine, which I continue to this day. I also peeled off the tape that was on my wrist and on my calf down to my ankle and balled it all up, bits of dust and hair stuck to the ends, then set it on the edge of the dirty bathtub. Last time I left it there like that, the tape got splashed with water and seemed to sort of take on new life. The rest of my tattoos are hidden by my dresses, so I don't have to tape them.

Several members of the troupe at the bar had tattoos—the girl with the most elaborate one, a wabori spread across her entire back, couldn't work without a shawl draped over her shoulders, but the other girls and I were adept at hiding ours with tape. I kept a large supply in my locker and if anyone forgot to bring their own, I would lend them some. When I was working every day, my reserve would dwindle surprisingly fast. Today there had been one new roll left in my locker, and I had given it to a younger troupe member who'd borrowed tape from me many times.

"Hey, I like the way your arm looks."

She always showed up for work with her short hair in a soto-hane flip style she did herself—maybe to economize on her beauty budget—and she said this as she tossed the tape into her own locker and gestured at the pattern that I wasn't really wild about but which obscured the burn scars on my upper arm. She herself had a long, thin tattoo of red spider lilies that extended from her inner wrist to her shoulder, and she would wind the tape around her arm so that, relative to the size of her tattoo, she used up quite a lot of tape.

"I really like the way those flowers are done with such fine lines. But I had to hide my burn scars."

She seemed fairly pleased by the compliment on her red spider lilies. I mean, it wasn't as if she had designed or inked them herself, but I honestly did think her tattoo was pretty and had even fleetingly considered getting something similar along my spine. The burns from my mother were only on my upper arm and shoulder. I had thought the scars would fade in time, but instead they became gradually more discolored, with the centers turning white—it was grotesque—so soon after I turned eighteen, I decided to cover them. At that point I was no longer living with my mother, but judging from her reaction when I later saw her, my tattoo didn't seem to upset her.

The lotus flower on the small of my back, the compass on my calf, and the rest were all just designs that struck my fancy, various whims. Having quit the bar, I thought now might be a good time to add a spider lily. Once you have one tattoo, it doesn't matter how many more you get—it has no further impact on the value of your body.

I run my hands over the spots where the tape was to make sure there isn't any adhesive residue, and when I turn off the hand shower, a sudden chill rushes to my core. I open the door to the bathroom and pull a bath towel from the shelf of clean linens above the washing machine, quickly drying myself off. I have to rub oil into the skin on the back of my arm while it's still damp, or else it gets taut and itchy, even after all this time. I don't know whether that's because of the burn or the tattoo. Once I've thoroughly applied it to my upper arm, I use the baby oil to moisturize the rest of my body. When I take a shower I'm like an automaton—I've been going through these motions for such a long time I bet I could be in a pitch-dark room or even have amnesia, no matter how distracted I was I'd still execute them perfectly. Although my body has cooled down after the flush from the hot shower, my face remains aglow, so I realize I must be drunker than I thought. But I've consumed far less alcohol than when I worked at the bar until closing time, let alone on those nights when I used to drink after getting off work or doing karaoke with the girls. What usually got me plastered was doing endless shots of sake or cheap shochu until morning, after I'd been drinking champagne or wine at work, so I blame my present state on going to the host club for the first time in a while.

The customer who happened to be at the bar left just before the end of the early shift, and I changed out of my dress back into the jeans I had been wearing then went for a quick drink at the club where the host who the woman from the bathhouse said now had Eri's dog worked. When Eri was still around here, one time she had persuaded me to tag along with her, and at first I couldn't remember the name of the relatively young host guy I had previously exchanged numbers with, but when we got to the club, it turned out he was the same guy Eri had requested as her shimei. Right after that, the young host had blown up my phone with texts and calls, and I felt sorry for him, but I hadn't ever requested him as my shimei for the night or my main shimei—the night we met I had simply chosen him to be the one to walk me to the elevators—so there was no problem, rules-wise. As soon as Eri and I sat down and I saw the young guy walking around the club, I'd remembered his name, but it wasn't worth worrying about.

"Ah, you're Eri's friend," said my shimei for the night, after striding over to where I sat. He was short, as was his hair, and he wore glasses, so he didn't look the part of a sought-after host, but here he was, in his thirties, working at one of this district's long-established clubs, so I figured he must have his share of clients.

"It's been a while."

"Did you go to the funeral? Ah, have they taken your order?"

"I went to the funeral, and they have not taken my order."

The host handed me the menu on the table and thanked me for coming. Eri had never been comfortable having a shimei host sit next to her, and now he took a seat on the side of the L-shaped sofa where I had set the shopping bag from the florist and my handbag, which put me at ease. A small bottle of shochu was included when you first requested a shimei, so I ordered jasmine tea as a mixer and lit my own cigarette, which I didn't feel like smoking. I don't much care for lighting custom-ers' cigarettes or having my own lit for me.

"The bar where you work, it's across the street from the local ward office, around the back, right? Did you just get off?"

The host lit his own cigarette, too, and from the stack of ashtrays on the table, he placed two in front of me and one in front of himself. Although he was short, his hands were large—his nails were groomed, he didn't bother with rings or bracelets—and for a host, he seemed to have good taste in watches. I had only rarely gone to clubs where the servers were male, usually accompanied by my male customers during after-time, though about three years back there was a local club where I used to occasionally stop in, but it had been a long time since I'd gone to a host club alone—I didn't know where to direct my gaze, so I just kept looking at the table.

"Yeah, I quit today. You have a good memory."

"Whaddya mean? Are you switching bars? Or moving? Ah, getting married or pregnant? Did you get in a fight with the manager? Changing jobs? Getting certified? Retiring to the countryside? Using your savings to move abroad? Making your debut as a singer for Sony Records?"

"Actually . . . my mother's sick . . . and I want to b— be with her."

"How many times have you used that one? I've worked here eight years and my grandma has died five times."

Another guy—pretty bland, I couldn't tell if he was a new host recruit or just regular staff—had brought over the tea and an ice pail, and my host deftly mixed the shochu with the jasmine tea for me. He didn't pester me with questions, instead he allowed the conversation to follow what I wanted to talk about, and I could tell he was a host with a range of topics at his disposal, none of which carried any whiff of discomfort or danger. Having said that, he didn't really seem to possess much in the way of masculine charm, and maybe what Eri had said about not seeing him as a man wasn't so hard to believe. On the verge of closing time, the club was raucous, with one young female patron shouting things into a microphone, and the host and I made innocuous conversation amid her rowdy outbursts but otherwise took advantage of the commotion to keep quiet, since it made our awkward pauses less so.

When the clamor rose to a particular level, with the music playing and whoever was chattering over the mike, the distance between the host and me inevitably shrank, but once the extreme noise subsided, we would automatically return to our original positions. It was just right for me—the pliant nature of this space shifting between us. My handbag remained in between us, but at some point the paper shopping bag had been set down on the other side of the host. He got up from his seat every so often, but he was never gone for long. As a flurry of last-call orders came in and customers were being sent off by their hosts, I kept my gaze on the table, trying to avoid looking around the frenetic club, unsure whether other customers who had also requested my shimei host were there that night. He was probably being attentive to me because I had just lost my friend.

"The dog."

The moment I spoke these words, a flamboyant host at another table started singing karaoke, so my host turned his ear toward me and leaned in close again. I could see that he had only one piercing and he wasn't wearing an earring, maybe the hole had closed up. It was too loud to get across complex sentences, but I couldn't just ignore the fact that he had leaned in, so I clearly sounded out the syllables, practically shouting, "Eri's dog!" As a sign that he'd heard what I said, the host kept his gaze forward and nodded emphatically, then he turned, bringing his face close to my ear, and rather than putting his arm around my shoulders, he slid it directly behind me on the back edge of the sofa and said, "I still have him, since I was taking care of him." My slender handbag was still at my hip, and though our bodies weren't touching, the outside of his thumb grazed the back of my upper arm.

There was an interlude in the karaoke, which meant the bellowing of the flamboyant host who had been singing stopped, and my host's face returned to its original position, but his arm remained behind me on the back of the sofa, at a slightly different angle, now bent at the elbow like a dogleg. As his hand moved away from my upper arm, I felt a tingle where my burn was.

"I sort of figured as much."

"He's a good dog. I mean, he's got a cheerful personality. A lot different from Eri."

I laughed. I'd only met Eri's dog once, and since I'd never had a dog myself, I had no basis for comparison, but the way he had kept looking at me expectantly, panting with his thin tongue hanging out of his mouth, had in fact seemed cheerful. It's odd that, despite spending plenty of time with Eri, hanging out in person and talking on the phone, my memories of the dog are more colorful than my memories of her.

"Did you want him? But he's already used to being at my house, so I guess I can't give him to you. Want to come see him?"

"I have no interest in owning a dog, my building doesn't allow it."

My reflexive avoidance of giving an answer about going to see it seemed to lend more weight to what had been a light-hearted, casual question. But the veteran host in his thirties said, "Well, if you want to see the dog, you can get in touch. Or if you just want to have a drink," opening and closing his cell phone, retrieving our text exchange.

"It's fine if she wanted to die, but c'mon, at least do it somewhere easy to get to. Not like Osaka."

"You mean like no further than Ikebukuro?"

"Sure, well, somewhere we could get to on the Yamanote line would be good."

"I got texts from her that said, 'I'm going to die now'—even on the day she actually died."

"Yeah. But I bet she also sent texts like that on days when she didn't die. Nothing to be done about it."

The interlude ended and the flamboyant host who had been quiet started bellowing again, so conveniently, I didn't have to say anything else. Whether that might have been *I guess so*, or *Yeah but*, or *Did you get those texts too?* I felt detached from any of these responses, so I preferred silence. The host remained silent too.

Just as the flamboyant host was finishing his karaoke number, my change from paying the bill arrived, so I stood up right away and reached for my purse and the paper shopping bag on the other side of my host, but he picked up my handbag before I could. "Let me do a little work. It'll make me feel like I've accomplished something," he said, scanning the entire club and leading me outside without passing me off to anyone else, so I followed him into the elevator. I had planned to walk home, but taking the mere three steps on the stairs from the elevator to the street, my legs felt a bit swollen and I was out of breath, so I caved and took a taxi. The host inquired which direction my place was and I told him, "It's straight up there and just to the left." Lately it's gotten to be especially tough, you have to fight for a taxi when it's closing time for all the bars and clubs in the district, but a young host who had been loitering out in front of the club managed to hastily summon a taxi for me from somewhere. It felt strange to hand money to my host, so I decided to just give the change from my bill to the driver and then quietly got into the taxi that had stopped a meter away. When I bent to get into the car, my host had put his hand lightly on my back and said, "Take care"—I think that was the only time he directly touched me.

I had taken a taxi so I wouldn't have to walk, but I still had to go around to the drugstore and the smoke shop and then climb the stairs to the third floor, so it felt

like I'd walked the same distance as I would have coming home from the club anyway, and as I stood before
the mirror applying toner to my face to quell its flush, I
had the urge to collapse onto the floor behind me. It was
cold in the apartment, and my body, wrapped in a towel,
was already freezing. The clothing that formed the pile
of laundry would soon be out of season, which seemed
to have happened quite suddenly. No matter where I
am, I feel no sense of reality. Not at the host club or in
my mother's hospital room—there is an inconsistency
between me and whatever scene I find myself in. Not
even the rooms where I live seem real to me, but so long
as the sounds of the door and the key ring out, I can feel
a small measure of security.

The next week sped by, now that I no longer had any
obligatory tasks other than visiting my mother's hospital
room, but my return home was always buoyed by the
subtle rhythm of the sound of the door followed by the
sound of the key. The first two days, I came straight
home from the hospital, and maybe because I wasn't
quite as physically exhausted, I couldn't sleep, so from
the third day on, I decided I ought to stop somewhere
or other before coming home. Mostly I killed time at
a bar that opened early or at a condo building in the
entertainment district where there was an online casi-
no. Then, after the weekend, there I am in a taxi from
the hospital coming straight home, and I find myself in
front of my apartment building thinking, *I just can't today
. . .* but right as I'm about to go around to the back, I

change my mind and figure I'll at least buy something to bring home, so I take a step backward, and when I turn around, I drop the key I have been gripping in my hand since I was in the taxi.

I bent down to pick up the key from the concrete, and crouching there for a few seconds, I changed my mind again and went around back of the building, where I pushed open the heavy door at the rear of the car park and ascended the interior staircase straight up to the third floor. Usually I don't run up the stairs. I hate breathing hard, and if I've been drinking it makes me nauseous. Today I haven't had a single drop. I haven't had any pills or sedatives or anything. With my momentum from running up the stairs, I heave my weight against the third-floor door, and sure enough, even when I burst through it like that, it still makes a dull creaking sound. Then, without waiting for the sensation of the usual rhythm, I put the key that's in my hand in the lock and turn it, and amid the clearly broken tempo of these two sounds, with the force of my body, I practically fall through the doorway. I lock the door behind me and put the key that's in my hand on top of the shoe cupboard, then I bend down, setting my handbag at my feet so I can take off my shoes.

There's no need to carry much with me when I go to the hospital. A smallish leather tote with a discreet brand logo, something not unreasonable for the hospital, that ordinarily doesn't hold much and that will spill its entire contents if I'm not careful. When I leave the house, I put the products I'll apply to my mother's face in a paper bag, and all that's in my purse is my wallet, phone, key, and a tiny pouch for cosmetics. Even when I'm not wearing much makeup, I hate not having anything with me to freshen up with.

When I arrived at the hospital room at ten in the morning, my mother was already awake, with the back-rest of her bed at a thirty-degree angle, and she was looking out the window with the questioning look of someone on narcotic painkillers in her eyes. I took some cotton and cheap toner out of the paper bag and set it on top of the fridge beside the bed, and without saying anything, I sat down in a folding chair and gazed in the same direction as my mother. Apart from occasionally muttering something I didn't quite understand or giving instructions about the angle of her bed or charging her phone, my mother didn't say much in particular either. Soon it's lunchtime, and while watching her pretend to eat her meal without consuming any of it, I myself eat half of the harusame noodle salad I bought at the convenience store on the first floor of the hospital when I got here. I had thought I'd be able to eat the whole thing, but the sight of the unpalatable hospital food ruined my appetite, as did the fact that, compared to my mother's emaciated arms, my own arms looked fat.

Although the drugs are working and my mother no longer complains about the pain, her breathing still seems labored. I can't tell if the wheezing is her intentionally trying to convey that she's suffering or if it's just the sound she's actually making. Nor can I tell whether my mother's bleary eyes and rambling words indicate that her mind isn't working properly, or that her eyes and lips are simply operating independently, and her mind and spirit are intact. Meanwhile, the woman from the bath-house and I have been texting. I don't mention that I went to see the host. On some level, I knew it was tacky to have done so. Our text exchange has drifted from the subject of Eri back to plans for cosmetic surgery and trashy manga. I also heard from a woman I used to work with at the bar, we were the same age and relatively close friends—there had been these two guys who used to request her and me, and now she was complaining that one of them had requested a twenty-year-old neither of us could stand.

I'd been sitting in the same posture for two days, fid-dling with my cell phone today, and yesterday flipping through—but not reading—various magazines I had bought, so not surprisingly, my lower back and legs were killing me, and I took advantage of my mother dozing off after her midday meds to duck out into the hallway. Just as I made it downstairs to go smoke a cigarette, my phone rang. The number came up as the hospital, so for a second I thought my mother had died, but they were call-ing to say she had a visitor. I told them I'd be right back, though since I was already on the first floor, I stepped out the entrance on the east side, took three puffs of a cigarette, and then reluctantly made an appearance at the nurses' station on the floor my mother's room was on, the floor where they put the terminal patients.

The man offered only his given name. It's rare for a guy who isn't a host to only use his given name. The man, who was clearly not a host, was probably in his late fifties or maybe about sixty, and I could tell from the clothing he wore that he was not only rich, but happy. He wasn't wearing anything over his fall jacket, and the only thing he was carrying was a small paper bag that he held by the folded-down top edge, so I figured he must have come here in his own car. Once my mother returned to the hospital after staying at my place, because she had complained in earnest about the pain and her trouble breathing, they had increased her dosage of narcotics, so basically she wasn't allowed visitors other than family, which meant that no one other than me went to see her. Meanwhile, prior to her stay at my place, it wasn't as if I had been at the hospital every day, and even when I was there it was only for a few hours, so someone else might have visited her, but I couldn't imagine who. There had only been the one time when I ran into a freelance editor who had helped my mother with her work.

As I started to explain to him about my mother's condition, the man nodded slowly without breaking his smile.

"I wasn't expecting to be able to see your mother."

And then, in quick succession, he followed with, I just wanted to give you this, as he offered the paper bag to me, its top edge, which had been folded closed, now open. *Don't take things from strangers*—the words popped into my head, I wasn't sure whether someone had actually taught me that phrase or it was just a cliché—but as my hands extended to approximately that same level, my eyebrows and the angle of my neck articulated doubt.

"I want you to have this. It belongs to your mother."

He showed no sign of withdrawing the paper bag and I was loath to get into a verbal tug-of-war in the hallway, with nurses coming and going, so for the time being I took hold of the paper bag—not by the handles but at its top edge—as a way of prompting an explanation about its contents. Perhaps sensing that I was understanding less than he had anticipated and likewise feeling this was an unsuitable place for a complicated interaction, he asked, May I speak to you for a moment? I went to my mother's room to check on her, and then led him to the hospital floor where there was a courtyard. He had not taken back the paper bag, so without knowing its contents but somewhat aware of its predictable weight, I carried it as we walked there.

"I first met your mother before you were born."

The weather was already cold enough that you needed a jacket, so there weren't many hospital patients or visitors walking around the courtyard, but several of the benches were already occupied. We found an appropriate bench, and as soon as we sat down—the man sitting beside me but at a remove—he turned to me and began talking.

"You may have heard of a bar called Conch."

My shoulders were a bit hunched even though I had on a light coat, but he didn't appear to feel the cold. The name of the bar he mentioned sounded familiar.

"My mother used to sing there."

"Yes, the bar had a little stage. As you say, your mother used to get up on that stage and sing her own original songs, I guess that's how she paid the bills. An actress in a theater company didn't make enough to eat. The bar itself was just your run-of-the-mill place where women waited on customers. But your mother was a radiant presence."

That bar's long gone now. Just as well, since my mother played it up as if it had been a hotbed of cultural exchange. I became aware of her delusion around the time I left home. Still, she had been fortunate. She saved the tips she earned as a nightclub singer and learned languages, taught small classes, and published several poetry collections—managing to support herself and have a kid without getting married. *Fortunate*—that was the word my mother herself used. I believed her expression of humility, at least in a literal sense.

An elderly woman in a wheelchair and her companion, sitting on a bench diagonally across from us, had stolen glances our way, so I became oddly self-conscious of where I was sitting beside the man. It made me laugh to imagine that, were they to listen in on our conversation, it might sound as if this was a daughter meeting her real father for the first time. I knew what my father looked like—he had seemed like a proud man, one who would envy others no matter what he himself possessed and whose ego seemed vulnerable. He would have been even older than the man sitting next to me on the bench. And he didn't have the whiff of wealth that this guy did. Without acknowledging who he was to me, my father had started coming to see me around the time I was in fifth grade, and would give me money.

My mother found out the following year and I was no longer able to see him. I didn't miss the middle-aged man who had suddenly appeared at that point in my life, but it was a drag not getting the money anymore. When I was in seventh grade, in junior high, I was the one who started going to see him—we met up a few times, but again, the following year, my mother found out. He died soon after I stopped seeing him the second time, when I was sixteen, and then when I turned seventeen I left the house where I lived with my mother.

"On the nights when your mother was there singing, I always tried to go to the club. I was a fan of hers. I also went to see her plays, but at those, I couldn't really get a good look at her, so the shows at Conch were precious to me because I'd be able to look at your mother up close. She really was a beautiful woman, and she had a great figure too. As her daughter, it might make you cringe to hear that."

The man laughed and the spot between his brows arched a little, but since I didn't respond in any particular way, he seemed to take that as a sign I was unbothered, so he shrugged and shook his head just slightly, raising his brows even higher. "Your mother was the kind of person who took pride in putting on a show," he said. For the customers' entertainment, the club would make her perform practically naked. My mother had evidently been offended by this, but, he said, there being limited forms of resistance available to her, she wore radical outfits when she sang. The closer to naked she was, the more lewdly the customers responded.

"She had the kind of shapely body men really like—pale and supple. I liked to think that I was her number-one fan, so it upset me to watch the drunken customers bantering with her, but the reality is, there I was, wanting to be with her myself, so I wasn't all that different from those vulgar drunks."

"You didn't hit on her? I mean, that's the kind of place it was, right?"

I was surprised to hear that my mother used to sing while half-naked, but it was kind of funny.

"The other girls who appeared on stage, they would sit with customers for tips when they weren't performing, and a lot of them worked in the bar as hostesses on days when they weren't on stage, but your mother, she didn't serve the customers—she would do her set and do a round of the tables to collect her tips, then she'd retreat backstage. To a guy like me, that made her seem all the more unattainable—I used to send her flowers all the time. I didn't have any money back then, you know, but I'd do whatever possible to give her as many tips as I could."

"High-handed of you."

The man had paused briefly in his story, so I interjected a brisk remark, but maybe because it came out louder than expected, the man let out a short chuckle. I didn't think of myself as high-handed, but I did seem to take pride in myself, he said with a laugh that was heartier than before, and he stood for a moment, tugged on the sleeves of his jacket to straighten it out, then sat back down again. When he was standing, the slanting sunlight had shone from behind his head, and his face had appeared dark for the moment it wasn't exposed to the sun. The weather had been fine all this past week but today the sunlight was particularly dazzling. In another month, winter will surely arrive. The doctor says that he doesn't know whether or not my mother will make it into the new year.

"Eventually your mother would quit singing at the bar, but before she did, there was one time when the two of us had a drink together."

It seems to me that, when the man sits back down, his position is just a little bit closer to where I am sitting than before, though I also find myself leaning forward just a little bit, so maybe it's my imagination. In any case, as the man continues his story, his face is now drawn closer than it had been at first.

"Not far from Conch, there was a place that served Italian food until late, and the two of us sat at the counter there talking, for about two hours. Up close, she truly was beautiful—her face was even more attractive than when you were seeing it from the stage, and her arms and neck were flawless—I really nursed my drinks so I wouldn't get drunk and forget it all. I knew it would be a waste not to remember every detail. Your mother didn't smile much, but that night she seemed to enjoy bad-mouthing Conch's owner and manager. She told me she was going to quit working there and I begged her not to, panicked at the thought of no longer being able to see her, but then I learned she had a boyfriend."

"The director who was almost twenty years older, with a family, whose wife used to be an actress too."

"Right—your father. But she told me she was thinking of breaking up with him. She must have found out she was pregnant right after that. She told me that when she quit the bar, she would also quit the theater—she had a job lined up. That's when I finally screwed up the courage to confess my feelings for her, but she let me down gently, saying she wanted to take some time to study and work."

I realize I need to check in on my mother. I've inadvertently been out here for quite some time. Besides, at the rate this guy is talking, there's no way to guess how much longer his story might go on. He's relaxed and maintains a semblance of being carefree, but there's also an impatience about him—whereas I have the sense that he's playing for time, it seems like he doesn't want the conversation to end abruptly. Meanwhile, the man who had been sitting diagonally in front of us and the elderly woman he brought out here in a wheelchair have gone, and now that I look around, there are only about half the number of people walking around the courtyard as there were previously.

I'd heard the details before—not from my mother but from my father. The story was so trite it seemed made up. My mother was the oldest of three daughters in a family that ran a small but well-established restaurant in a backcountry town—though it wasn't so far from central Tokyo—where, fed up with the pressure to take a husband, with the backcountry, and with the dingy restaurant her family took such pride in, she fled to the city where glorious "culture" was in full bloom and auditioned to become a member of a theater company. The director and head of the company—my father—was the kind of cad who, despite already having a family of his own, would often mess around with the women in his company; from the moment he set eyes on my mother, he took an immediate liking to her, and they were soon an item. He considered divorce for a time, but he wasn't the hot-blooded type who could toss aside his two children and a wife who never gave him a whit of aggravation. My father didn't strike me in the least as a ladies' man, but either he just had a way with women or he really applied himself—apparently he'd had quite the panoply of lovers. There did not, however, seem to be any other children born outside his family. My mother refused to allow my father to assuage his feelings of guilt by giving her money—with the exception of maternity expenses, she didn't accept any support from him. Not that he had much money to speak of in the first place.

At the end of the summer of my second year in junior high, when I called the phone number my father had given me and saw him again for the first time in over a year, he was saddened by the terrible burns on my arm. Without me having to say a word, he guessed that they were my mother's doing. I saw no reason to deny the fact to my fearsome father, nor did I dare to. It's not that your mom hates you—it's my fault, he lamented. I came to see you knowing that she would never allow it. Your mom has always been afraid of losing things, he added.

This alleged fear of my mother's, I wasn't sure whether it was about losing me to my father, or about losing him to me. Had I dug any further, I knew I would have gotten nothing more than his own take on it, so I didn't bother to ask—besides, I was convinced that both were incorrect.

I have no memories of my mother beating me or yelling at me. At the beginning of my second year in junior high, not long after we switched to summer uniforms, I would kill time at a local hangout with my friend and some older boys she knew, and when I came home late one night, my mother was sitting in front of her word processor staring out the window, and she seemed awfully surprised to see me. I was already staying out nights or coming home in the wee hours, so I'm certain she wasn't surprised about what time it was. My friends and I had learned to avoid getting caught for being out late at night or going to places where we could drink by changing into regular clothes in train station bathrooms or at someone's house. It wasn't every day, though it happened often enough that seeing me with a flushed face or in clothes that were unfamiliar to her wouldn't have surprised my mother. I told her that I had been at a friend's house, and after exchanging a few more words, I tried to head toward the bathroom—at that moment, my mother grabbed my arm and pressed her burning cigarette into the area just above my elbow. An involuntary yelp emanated from the back of my throat at the same time that I reflexively tried to pull my arm away, at which point the cigarette slid upward across my skin before burning out and falling to the floor, but my mother's grip on my arm grew stronger. Sharp pain coursed through me instantly, and as I looked at my mother's fingers digging into my arm, it felt like she was tethering rather than grasping me.

Various options raced through my mind, I think—should I flee? Cling to her? Or make some kind of noise? However, my body had surrendered all movement. My mother wasn't looking at my face. Her eyes were on my arm, and she brought the heavy silver lighter next to her word processor near my arm and lit it—the sleeve of the cheap, skintight T-shirt I was wearing ignited in a fraction of a second, producing an awful smell and clinging to my skin as it went up in flames. When skin burns, even if only for a moment, it gives off an animal smell. Had my mother—who may not have expected the flames and who seemed surprised by my screaming—had she not immediately thrown her half-drunk coffee on me, my entire upper body probably would have been burned where it was covered by the T-shirt. When I looked at my mother, she still wore an expression of surprise, but a little while later, she put me under a cool shower in the bathroom and then took me to the overnight clinic at a big hospital. The burns blistered many times and itched like crazy, and afterward the spot where the cigarette had first been pressed to my arm and the area where the T-shirt had touched my skin formed separate lesions that left their own scars.

"The girls at that club, they all had a little glint in their eyes, as if they were waiting for their chance. Like they believed their chance to move on, from where they were to somewhere else, would be found among their none-too-bright customers."

The way the man described those women seemed completely different from how the women I knew who worked at bars appeared. I, for one, had never seen anything other than money reflected in a customer's face. I'm not sure if it's simply revisionist memory on his part, or if it has something to do with the time and place, or if that's how it really looks from the customer's perspective.

"While some girls batted their eyelashes, there were also girls who greedily asked for favors, and others who promoted their talents. Even to a punk like me, without any clout at all back then. I think quite a few of them would sidle up to customers to get acquainted, pretending as if they were willing to give up their bodies for money. There were some girls who definitely seemed to turn tricks almost every night. I wonder where those girls ended up. Your mother was a cool one but she was talented, and maybe she was looking for a toehold somewhere, a way out of her day-to-day with the small theater company and the affair. But she was sensible enough to know that kind of toehold wasn't to be found in a place like that. That's why she left."

A woman younger than my mother whose unvarying gaze seemed to lack a focal point—like my mother's in the hospital room—was being pushed in a wheelchair by a man who appeared to be her husband, and they had approached, heading toward us from the middle of the courtyard. I had also pushed my mother's wheel-chair around this courtyard many times, but she didn't seem to like this artificial kind of landscape, so she had soon started pretending that she was tired. My mother must have held genuine contempt for the club's pseudo-prostitute hostesses. As well as, of course, the men who were there to buy them, who also seemed to think they could buy my mother.

The man turned my way, and his expression was a bit dazzled. He had the look peculiar to those who live a good life, with a discerning eye for things. I wondered if he was imagining the desolate place where I live. And naturally I was concerned about how my mother was doing. I made a show of opening my cell phone to check the time, and the man said, Shall we go back? I respond-ed by suggesting that we could talk a bit longer as we walked. It wasn't just that I was worried about my moth-er—although the now quite oblique sunlight was still shining in the courtyard, I was feeling chilled.

While we were waiting for the elevator, the man said something to the effect that he felt like my mother seemed to sort of hate her own beauty.

"When we were drinking at that Italian place, she had spoken derisively about another singer, a woman who was the lover of someone important at Conch. That's why they let her perform, she said. Your mother went on to say, with vehemence, that this other girl dressed far more respectably when she sang—not because she was such a good singer, but because she had an ugly birthmark on her back. Being admired by men is a disadvantage. Men treat pretty women as showpieces, while they love ugly women in secret. That was your mother's unique perspective on it."

The first elevator was full of mostly hospital staff and carts, so we waited for the next one, and when it finally arrived, the man broke off for a moment and I quickly got on, while he seemed discreetly aware of his surroundings. I had really wanted to go downstairs to smoke a cigarette before returning.

"She may very well have been right. You probably know yourself, since you're gorgeous like your mother. After she quit the bar and had a child on her own—I don't think your father knew about this—it was really a struggle for her to get back to feeling like herself again. Her savings dipped, and her job prospects must have dwindled. She would call me on the phone once in a while. She wanted to go back to singing at the bar like before, and she would have, but they had told her that now she'd have to work as a hostess too. She'd had it with being made to sing with barely any clothes on. If, as they say, necessity knows no law, before long she'd end up sleeping with those men, and she cried to me and said that what scared her was being forced to attach a specific price to her body. At the time, I had just set up my own business and didn't have much money to spare, but I was willing to lend her whatever she needed and to offer what help I could."

The elevator soon arrived at the floor my mother's room was on, after stopping twice along the way. It was only while a nurse had gotten on and then off again at the next floor that the man had paused his story and then instinctively resumed it. He stopped once again, and even though he and I were the only ones on the elevator, he held the door open for me to get off and then cautiously stepped off himself. With apparently no intention of coming to my mother's hospital room, he stopped and stood at the elevator bank.

"Maybe your mother was too much of a good girl. She seemed to have so much pride, but either she wasn't the type to turn bad, or she was destabilized from having just had a baby. I was so naive, though, she could have cheated me out of however much she wanted and left me drowning in debt. I used to see her from time to time, but she'd say that she wouldn't take any help, or that she couldn't imagine being bought by a man, kept in a box or selected to be displayed on a shelf with other women—she'd rather do the hustling herself. She wasn't in love with me. But she did love your father."

For some reason, there had been steady traffic on the elevators, and since we had been standing there, the elevator hall had gradually filled with people. Visitors on their way home, doctors and hospital staff, pajama-clad patients perhaps on their way to buy something at the shop—their eyes scanned the indicator lights above the elevators.

"It's against the rules for me to tell these things to you, her daughter. Still, the relationship we had continued, on-again, off-again, even after I got married, but eventually, without things ever really coming to an end, it seems that your mother became unable to keep in touch by phone or text."

The man's voice had dropped to a whisper in the crowded corridor, but now it seemed to have grown just a bit louder. "I thought she had longer to live," he said, at a volume that wouldn't travel more than a few meters amid the noise but that nonetheless had the timbre of a shout.

"I thought she'd live a little longer, so I hope you'll accept this money, it's what I intended to give her for the time she had left. I won't come again. Were I to see your mother's face, I don't think I'd be able to leave her side, not until she took her last breath. She would never allow herself to be watched over by the likes of me, someone who bought her with money. She has too much pride. She wouldn't let a customer keep vigil."

The man lightly grasped my hand with the paper bag in it, and I was surprised by the warmth of his hands. My own hands were ice-cold from the early-winter air, and it would take some time before they returned to normal temperature.

The abbreviated interval between the creak of the door and the key turning in the lock still echoed in my ears as I cast a glance around the desolate table, pulled off my low-heeled booties, and, from the handbag I had set down at my feet, took out the paper bag with its top folded down. A lot of customers at the bars in this district paid in cash rather than running a tab or using a credit card. So I was used to seeing wads of bills and could usually tell the amount by their weight and bulk. But I hadn't wanted to open the bag in the hospital room with my mother, even if her gaze was unfocused. I folded my legs under me and sat on my heels, right there in the entryway, and looked at the four thick banking envelopes that had been inside the paper bag, taking one and opening it to see that there were two stacks of one million yen, each with bank tape wrapped around it. I stuck my hand inside the bag and touched the other envelopes— they all seemed to be the same thickness.

When I had returned to my mother's room, she had already woken up and was breathing audibly, her mouth open as she stared at me without speaking. Either she intentionally made a noise or else the sound escaped from her throat while she was wheezing, but a couple of times I could hear what seemed like a groan. I drew closer and used the remote control to lower the reclining angle of her bed a little, but she grumbled as if to imply this was no good, so then I raised it a bit, which brought no complaint, and the sound of her breathing did seem more at ease, if only slightly. I had often been uncertain about what my mother was thinking, even before her illness robbed her of most of her words. Her mood will change inexplicably sometimes, and she can be stubborn about the strangest things. Despite that, I still know her better than I know anyone else, and that remains true even now that she's lost the ability to speak.

Although according to the calendar it's too soon to call it winter, the sun is setting much earlier, and when

I'd been in the courtyard, the air had the hue of noon-time, but back in the hospital room, the light outside the window has a slightly warmer tone, and the sunlight that shines in on part of the bed even more so.

"The days have gotten shorter."

Perched on the utmost edge of my mother's bed, rather than in the chair, I spoke without expecting her to respond. Since my mother had returned to the hospital, while at times she could manage to reply with a *yes* or *right*, other times she didn't answer at all or said strange things very loudly. She no longer had the facility to keep up appearances with excessively self-conscious, poetic phrases, the way she used to.

"Yes, they have."

At this unexpected and clearly enunciated reply, I peered directly at my mother's face rather than gazing at her sidelong as I had been, but it appeared to have been more of a reflexive reaction than a deliberate response—sure enough, the focus of her eyes was fluctuating somewhere indeterminate.

"A man came by."

"Oh."

"He gave me money."

"Oh."

"We were even poorer than I thought?"

"Right."

"Then you should have married that guy."

"Yes."

"Aside from the fact that you had a kid with someone else, you could have been like any other rich and well-kept wife. You wouldn't have had anything to hide, you wouldn't have had to sing half-naked, and you probably wouldn't have gotten sick. You could have written as much poetry as you liked, whether it made you any money or not."

I rattled on, knowing there was no longer any meaning attached to my mother's reactions. Never in my life had I asked her so many questions. My mother would occasionally pepper me with questions, but I hardly ever asked her about anything. Will you be home tomorrow night? Why doesn't my father live with us? How much do you make from language classes and selling your poetry collections? Why do you put on makeup and wear stockings even when you're not going to see anybody else? How come you don't get angry about me smoking and drinking? Why am I not allowed to see my father? Do you know what kind of work I do in this district? Do you know when I'm lying to you? Why did you burn me instead of beating me or kicking me out? I hadn't asked her any of these questions.

"Right after I got my period for the first time, my friend from junior high who went with me to buy pads gave me condoms for some reason and I put them in my bag, but the next morning they were gone. Did you throw them away?"

My mother's reactions had grown sluggish, and her eyes were halfway closed, so I tried asking something from among the unasked questions that didn't have any particular significance or meaning attached to it. Sure enough, there was no response. I picked up the remote control, now sandwiched between the mattress and the bedframe, and brought my mother's position a little more parallel to the floor. This time my mother uttered nothing about whether she was comfortable or not. A nurse arrived with dinner and I half stood to take the tray from her, bringing the table in front of my mother and setting it down there for now, though she wasn't going to eat it anyway. I then sat back down, taking up as little territory as possible on the edge of the bed.

"I guess my burn doesn't really have anything to do with my father, does it?"

My mother, having only barely brushed the meal tray with her fingers, not even touching the hot tea, now had her head slightly askew on the pillow and had closed her eyes. I had spoken those words even more softly, so she would have barely been able to hear me. My mother did not open her eyes. Before long, a nurse brought in my mother's medications, and my mother half opened her eyes to take her meds, then she went back to sleeping, her brow still furrowed.

Had it been her own skin that my mother wanted to burn? Or rather, was it that my skin, which had been created from her own body, was her skin too? I opened the other envelopes for the briefest glimpse inside to check the size of the wads, and I realized that I didn't have a drawer that locked or a safe in my apartment. Up until now, I had never brought home any sum that amounted to more than a month's salary, not counting the daily wage, and even that had fines and the cost of hair and makeup deducted from it, and nothing else here was expensive or valuable.

My body heavy and stiff, I haul myself up from the entryway, set the paper bag on the low table, and, putting my purse down beside me, sit on a cushion on the floor and light a cigarette. The floor is even colder than it was last week, and I debate whether to turn on the heat, deciding not to for the time being, instead keeping my coat on, and I take my cell phone out of my now practically empty purse.

—BTW, you working today?

I send a message to the woman from the bath-house. I take the lip balm I had tossed into the now-otherwise-empty pachinko-prize paper box the day before and rub it into the inner part of my lips, which are a little chapped, and soon her reply comes in.

—At work. But it's slow. Pretty dead here so looks like I'll get off right at midnight.

—Wanna get a drink? Or something to eat.

—Well, I could get a bite to eat but starting today I work four days straight, on again tomorrow morning.

—What time again in the morning? 10?

—Right.

Her texts came back straightaway so it must have really been dead there. She was a hard worker, no doubt she came from a home with both parents, although they lived somewhere you've never heard of, in some hick town outside Tokyo in Chiba or Saitama, not the kind of place many people manage to make it out of for the big city. She goes to work in the old red-light district four or more often six days a week, and when she has her period she probably works at a different place where she doesn't have to do the deed. I bet her monthly take is close to three times what I had been making, working in a bar six nights a week.

—I feel like drinking so I'll hit you up again after your 4-day stretch.

—What's up with you—not enough booze since you quit the bar?

—Just that I got some extra cash and these days I can't sleep when I come home anyway.

—Oh, what happened with the S&M?

Until she mentioned it, I had forgotten about the dominatrix sex club she had gone to the trouble of sending me the contact information for. At Eri's funeral, there had been a pervading and inexplicable sadness that seemed to lament her life rather than her death, and I had just been curious to know a little more about her. The sex clubs where she had worked in Osaka or its suburbs were probably run-of-the-mill, and I doubted they would open any particular doors into the S&M world, but my intention in asking about them had to do with the fact that I was unlikely to fail the interview at one of those places because of the burns on my body or my tattoos. Bathhouses and sex clubs that pay half-decently frown upon body scars that predate facial sculpting. In addition to having tooth implants, Eri had an array of cutting scars, each the same depth, that ran along the inside of her left arm from the wrist to the elbow. I did them when I was young, she had said, but she'd been young even when she died.

—Haven't gone yet. I spend all my days at the hospital. Tattoos are okay for S&M?

I asked this casually, even though I hadn't looked into it at all myself—maybe it was the momentum from the barrage of questions I had directed at my mother, who may or may not still understand. I hadn't screwed the cap back on the tube of lip balm very well, so I put some more on the tip of my finger and rubbed it into my lips, which were still sticky from the previous application.

—These days you see a lot of call girls with them. Only place they're no good is at cheesy hot springs that have family-friendly pools attached.

I touch my left arm with my right hand, circling my fingers from my outer arm toward the inside, gently tracing the subtle unevenness through my clothes. The artist who inked my tattoo had been a woman—she was courteous and without a doubt skilled, and had worked in a big, bright tattoo parlor on a busy street in an area that was frequented by junior high and high school students. Rather than create designs herself, she preferred to work from drawings or photographs customers brought in with them, inking tattoos that accurately and beautifully reflected their requests, so I showed her a few motifs from a tattoo magazine that she diligently followed, even using a variety of black tones in somewhat atypical ways where my burn scars were, thus rendering them completely inconspicuous. I ran my fingers over the same spot repeatedly, my fingers remembering the extra texture there, until it felt as though the unevenness was practically gone. And when I touched the places I had tattoos where there weren't scars, like where there were thick black lines, the texture felt a bit like welts.

—I'm going out drinking. Maybe I'll go see that host.

—LOL. You should take advantage of those street touts and go begging for a shokai, instead of wasting your money on some guy!

I acknowledged the message from the woman from the bathhouse, and then I texted the host that had been Eri's shimei. I didn't know how often he checked his messages while he was working. If I didn't hear back from him, I could do like the bathhouse woman said and just drink at some club for the newbie price of three or five thousand yen. I had already roused myself while I was still typing the text.

I hadn't washed my hands yet since coming home, so I went to the bathroom, washed my hands with soap and dried them with the well-worn bath towel left on top of the washing machine, then brought my face close to the mirror to check if my makeup was cakey. I took the folding mirror and ceramic curling iron and went back out to sit on the floor in front of the table. If the lighting isn't bright enough, my makeup tends to be too heavy, but when I'm going out at night, heavy make-up is a good thing. I shoved a stick with a bunch of Asian lettering on it up my nose to perk myself up, and then I added a few pencil strokes to the inner corners of my eyebrows. Originally the inhaler stick just contained menthol, but there's a Chinese dude who sells it with some other powder in it. As I wiped caked makeup from the outer corners of my eyes with a cotton swab, I tried to remember when I met him—I'm sure it was through someone who worked for one of Eri's customers.

My phone rang. It was the host.

"Good morning, what's up?"

"Wait, you're not at the club now?"

The sound in the background is definitely not that of the host club. The singer of a rock band that was wildly successful about a decade ago is singing an unfamiliar song. I can't tell if it's a new song or an old album playing.

"At the salon. I came in thinking I'd get a haircut but the stylist told me I've got grays so I'm getting it dyed, which takes forever. Guess I'll be fashionably late."

The salon must be in this neighborhood. At this hour any type of business can be bustling—whether it's a hair or nail salon, or even a restaurant serving grilled beef tongue. I dared to be like the sitting duck in the proverb, walking in with a leek on my back, ready to be cooked.

"I'll come for a drink, what time will you get to the club? We could even meet up and go there together. I'm drinking tequila and champagne."

"Why—did something happen?"

The host's voice was light and cordial, rather than grave or amused. A veteran, he's on guard upon encountering a leek-bearing duck, neither fazed nor keyed up by it. In the short breaks in our conversation, I could hear the music even more clearly. I strained my ears to focus on the lyrics only to be put off when I heard my name being likened to an angel.

"I can't think of a place to go drinking. What time will you be at the club?" I persisted, aware that he was on guard.

"Do you want to talk outside?"

"The club is fine. The louder the better, actually."

"I'm done here, but the salon is near the station so it'll take me about thirty minutes."

The host sounded acquiescent so I hung up and, using the pad of my finger, smeared some glittery eyeshadow onto my lids. The voice of the rock singer echoed in my head, more so than the host's, but I don't have anything in my apartment for playing music to block it out. The heap of cigarette butts in the ashtray was close to spilling over, and the cigarette I put out before had ignited one of the old butts, which was smoldering a little. I opened a plastic bottle that had been under the table since who knows when and poured some water over it to extinguish the smoke. It stunk but I was going out so I didn't care. I put two of the envelopes the man gave me on the shelf under the kitchen sink, and another one in the drawer under my bed where I keep my underwear, then I opened the last one and started to take out one of the stacks of bills, but on second thought, I stuffed it back in and put the envelope with both stacks in my purse. I'd be nervous to walk around carrying eight million yen, but two million is fine. This district is rife with women walking around with two million yen. Nearly the same number who say they want to die.

In an attempt to make up for the earlier broken rhythm, and with the sound of the rock band still playing in my head, I turned the key in the lock, and while that sound still echoed, I firmly pulled open the door that leads to the staircase, making a metallic creak. Even though pulling versus pushing the door created a different effect, it followed a much more regular rhythm than before. As I hurried down the stairs, any sense of guilt, which I hadn't felt in a long time, was drowned out by the clicking of my heels.

With the right side of my body, I heave my weight against the door, which gives with unexpected momentum as it swings open. That momentum propels me to step forward into the carpeted corridor, and when I let go of the door, it closes with painstaking yet deliberate slowness so as not to make a sound. Ultimately, the gentle, elegant noise it does emit serves to inform that the door has fully closed. I walk down the corridor, where my heels are silent, and sticking out the knuckle of my middle finger, I push the lower of two buttons in between the two elevators. A barely perceptible sound signifies that an elevator has responded and is heading toward this floor, and after a short wait, a flat mechanical sound indicates its arrival. The interior of the elevator floor is cushioned with a rubbery material—no sound from my heels.

It had been a long time since I left for the hospital from a place other than my own apartment. Before my mother came to stay with me, when she was still able to change her own underwear and get up—albeit slowly—to use the en-suite toilet in her room, I would arrive from the nail salon or a restaurant. Since she'd returned to the hospital, when I went straight there in the mornings, leaving was always preceded by the creak of the door and the click of my heels on the stairs.

I waited impatiently for each of the two automatic glass doors, with an intercom in between, to open, and when I stepped out onto the sidewalk of the avenue, I noticed the remarkable amount of dog hair stuck to my skirt, so I stood there for a moment and brushed it off with my hand. The host lived two stops away from the district where his club was, on the west side of the station. I had gotten here by taxi, but I knew this street—what's more, I knew exactly how to get to the station. I used to live on the east side of the station, with my mother. Compared to the west side, with its new condominiums lining the wide avenues, all the streets on the east side were old and run down, with nothing worth mentioning about them other than how cheap the rent was for a location that could be considered within central Tokyo—albeit just barely. My elementary school had been on the east side and my junior high school on the west side; my housewife friend who had disappeared with another man—she grew up on the east side, but she had been living on the west side in a condo her husband had bought.

"How come you live there? Isn't it out of the way?"

I had asked this of the host after ordering a third round of five-shot sets of tequila, when my peripheral vision had gotten pretty blurry. A couple of young hosts had joined us to drink tequila but neither of them were making much conversation, so I ended up talking the whole time to the veteran host, Eri's "consultant." It seemed like one of his shimei clients had shown up, but apparently he sent her home before the club closed, when I was leaving.

"If it were closer to the club, these guys would crash there all the time," the host said, gesturing casually at the younger ones. One of them started talking, prattling on about how he'd been a couch surfer at the previous place, how that apartment had been awesome and how he wished the host would get another place nearby, but he'd also been to where he lives now and that place was nice, and so on and so forth—I lost interest in hearing any more details. What I was asking about wasn't why he lived so far from the club, I wanted to know why he chose to live in that particular neighborhood.

The quickest way to get from the avenue to the station would be to turn at the corner where the big supermarket is and take the narrow street lined with convenience stores and pachinko parlors. But for some reason I decided to continue along the avenue, turning at the crossroad and going over the railroad crossing in order to pass through the jumble of streets on the east side of the station. I anticipated that the railroad crossing wouldn't be open—it never was—but as it came into view, the gate arm swung open as if it had been waiting for me, and I headed east almost without having to break my stride. A few familiar shops were still there, a few new chain stores had appeared, and a few storefronts were shuttered.

Further east there's an elementary school, and if you climb the hill beyond that, it's not far to my mother's apartment—probably still full of her things—but I turned right onto a narrow street that ran parallel to the tracks and headed toward the station. I have a key to her place, but I don't carry it with me. I grew up in that rather nondescript two-room apartment—one room has a tatami floor and the other, gray carpeting—just about the same size as the one I live in now. My mother's desk and bookshelves were in the carpeted room that had a small balcony attached. In the tatami room, there was a low table where we ate our meals and where I did my homework, and at night we pushed it aside and laid out our futons. The two rooms were separated by just a sliding door, so there was no wasted space at all, and a small kitchen was connected to the tatami room, with the front door located on the other side. Only in the dead of winter did we have to use a balanced flue to fill the bathtub, and otherwise, the apartment had excellent exposure. My memories from when I was little are flooded with bright sunlight.

The thin sliding door didn't require much effort to open, but my mother would sometimes sequester herself behind it when she was working—leaving it open basically made the two rooms feel like one. Up until I started elementary school, I never saw that door closed, so my mother may have detached it and put it away somewhere. I never had a curfew, nor was I ever forced to take extracurriculars or pursue a certain career path, as many of my classmates were. Eventually that thin sliding door, easily opened at any time, became insufficient, and I started spending more time out at night with my friends. I might sometimes get nagged about my clothes, but even when it was obvious I was doing things like smoking and shoplifting, my mother didn't seem all that surprised or angry. Thinking back on occasional snippets of conversation, however, it's perfectly clear to me the kind of women she held in contempt and the kind of money she had a distaste for.

Since leaving home at seventeen, I had rarely been back to the apartment where I'd lived with my mother. I hadn't taken up much space, so I figured my mother lived on her own there with the furniture arranged pretty much the same. The sliding door has probably been taken off.

The stores became closer together and the shuttered storefronts dwindled, and as the streets approached the bustle of the area in front of the station, I recognized the greengrocer on the left corner.

The merchandising at the front is like that of any fruit and vegetable shop in a shopping district, though what's on offer is the kind of relatively upscale yet somehow lackluster fruit meant for gift-giving and those unusual vegetables used only in Chinese cooking. A young couple who probably live on the west side wearing shiny and new leather jackets are browsing the storefront. There's a greengrocer at the entrance to the entertainment district where I live and also one in front of the station nearest there. The one in the entertainment district sells fruit skewered on sticks to young people at a huge markup, while the one by the station takes the price-gouging to another level, selling beautifully cut fruit and cakes to the women who come to shop at the department stores. This shop is not like either one of those. It's been here forever.

A thin middle-aged lady is sitting in a chair at a small table at the front of the store—she used to sit there tapping her ashes into an ashtray on the table and, whether from poor health or poor temper, never smiling. She's still sitting there, looking almost exactly the same as when I was in junior high, only older by that many years. I see that the ashtray is missing from the table—whether out of mindfulness for her wellbeing or local ordinances—and in its place is a sort of simple cash register made up of cans, the contents of which she is counting. The lady has a magazine on her lap, and while she's not quite flashy, her face is not entirely free of makeup. This also tracks with my memory of her. She doesn't have a manicure but her eyebrows are penciled, and perhaps because she's slender, she still bears a vestige of sexuality.

As far as I know—as someone who lived along these streets my whole life—she's always been here, she's always been middle-aged, and she's always been skinny. When I think of this station, the first image that comes to mind is this fruit and vegetable shop, and when I think of this shop, all I see is this lady. When I was younger I never bought fancy fruit, and my mother hated this shop. Realizing I could buy fresh-squeezed fruit juice, I thought about bringing it to the hospital, or I could buy gelatin with fruit in it, and as I was thinking this and peeking inside the shop, from out of nowhere a man in his thirties wearing a suit and shopping for fruit came up diagonally behind me, asking in a brash voice, "Mother, can you make up an assortment for the same price as last time but with different stuff?" Without so much as a smile, the lady directed him to a young employee, who asked the man in the suit a number of questions as he swiftly assembled a box.

I headed toward the station, not having bought anything or said a word, my pace faster than intended. Now, at a fast walk that was almost a jog, my inner thighs felt funny. It must have been from where they came in contact with the host's hipbones. I remember having sex but I don't remember whether he came or not. I'd been worried about quelling the nausea and not throwing up on his clean, navy-blue sheets, so I hadn't come, but the sensation that spread from my vagina at the moment of penetration had felt good—it'd been a while. He'd told me that he and Eri never had sex. I wasn't inclined to believe what the host said in general, but that had been my impression anyway.

By the time we finished drinking the tequila, it was already past last call, and the figure on the bill the in-house guy brought over was less than one hundred thousand, so rather than open the envelope, I took cash out of my wallet to pay, leaving the envelope buried at the bottom of my bag. Considering the table charge, the beer, shochu, and mixers we drank along with the tequila, plus the inexplicable service and shimei fees that are appended at this sort of club, I had the feeling there may have been a slight discount since the last time, but then again it was probably just the correct amount—if there was discount, it was so minor I didn't dare question it. Maybe because of the powder I had snuffed right before going out, I had been drunk enough that I bumped my shoulder against the elevator door and the host had escorted me out, probably skipping out on the club's after-hours meeting, and I have no memory of what I said to him, though I must have used the excuse of going to see the dog to have ended up at his place. When I woke up there, I didn't have any particular sense of doubt or regret, though I felt a strange ache on the left side of my head.

Walking along at such a sprint, I soon arrived at the station and fished in my bag for my IC card, but since I used it so seldomly, it was nowhere to be found. The envelope at the bottom of my bag still held the stacks of bills. When I was using his shower, the host had woken up and offered to walk me to the station, but I had demurred. Then, while he was taking a shower, I made sure the wads were there, feeling a twinge of guilt as I did so. The dog that I had met at Eri's place had panted, his thin little tongue wagging expectantly and his eyes shining with hope that there was something in my bag. I have no choice but to buy a ticket, so I check the fare to the station closest to the hospital where my mother awaits death and jostle onto the train for the first time in months. The last train I took was for Eri's funeral.

I assume that my mother can no longer taste even juice or gelatin, but thinking she might have taken some slight pleasure in the juice, I regret not having bought any for her. I can still hear the voice of the man in the suit who was not her son, brazenly calling out *Mother* to the middle-aged lady. My mother may have hated that shop, though I doubt she would have noticed the juice had come from there. But I had not been raised to call people who were not my mother *Mother*. The word, connoting the parent who had once held dominion over my body, carries too much meaning. My mother, born in the early months of the year, would likely die before she turned fifty-four. I will have to cremate my fifty-three-year-old mother, whose skin and hair show the tragic ravages of an old woman. Her skin and blood and flesh will surely vanish in the flames, but her bones will remain—along with her teeth, I imagine.

The train that runs above ground doesn't stop at the station closest to the hospital, so I decide to walk the fifteen minutes there. I considered taking a taxi, but as I rode the wave of people peculiar to the morning time, I continued past the taxi stand. Were it not for my frequent visits to the hospital, I'd never have any reason, at this hour, to breathe the air outside of the neighborhood where I live. Now that my housewife friend—she was an early riser—is gone, I can't think of a hypothetical situation that would necessitate such. Among the things my mother had bestowed upon me were a perfectly healthy body, the scars that had slashed the value of that body by half, and, in the dwindling bloom of my twenties, time to waste walking in the languid morning. In front of me are several middle-aged men in suits earnestly going

81

about their lives, and crows, and a vehicle for the con-
tractor that restocks vending machines, and a squashed
can of coffee apparently run over by that vehicle—this
truly unevocative scene has been granted to me by my
ailing mother.

In the hospital's lobby, I go through the process I've
been through countless times to get a visitor's badge, and
as I take one of the many elevators, standing in front of
the panel of buttons with numbers on them, a pair of
women who get on after me and quickly move all the
way to the back proceed to speak in a cheeky drawl from
someplace a bit west of here—do they or don't they realize I can hear them?—making comments about the
tattoo on my left wrist. "But Akashi-san's son also had a
tattoo, and when he came to the funeral, he brought his
children along." "Did he now?" These were their part-
ing lines as they stepped off the elevator on the seventh
floor. One of them was carrying flowers, the other, a
paper shopping bag from an upscale fruit shop.

The elevator started moving again and I had the sensation of the air in my body being pulled downward,
which persisted as I arrived at the floor where my mother's room was. A nurse I recognized had been standing
there at the elevator bank and I nodded to her, then
headed toward my mother's room, walking briskly so no
one could look at me too closely. The ridiculous clicking of my heels down the corridor was sort of amusing.
I had showered at the host's apartment without washing my hair. Here in the disinfected air of the hospital,
my hair reeked of alcohol and cigarettes. But if I use

any perfume, it makes my mother unbearably nauseous, and I myself—still queasy from last night—can't take any strong smells either.

The door to my mother's room was open, and from the way one nurse was standing with her back to me, I could tell there were more people inside. I slowed my walking and approached the nearest nurse, deliberately rustling my bag to draw her attention to my presence. My mother hadn't died—she had been making a troubling sound in her throat, and so it seemed the doctor was suctioning out phlegm. It was the same doctor who had been in charge and consulted with us on the day my mother arrived at the hospital for this stay, when I had accompanied her in the taxi.

"The phlegm isn't causing her difficulty breathing, it's the fact that she has lost the strength to cough it up herself, so periodically we'll suction what we can. The nurse will take care of it next time."

The doctor had taken what appeared to be the suction device from my mother's mouth and set it on a silver tray, looking me in the face and then looking downward before meeting my gaze again and explaining this. I murmured a vague thank-you—it felt odd to express gratitude, but I had no other vocabulary in response— and when I made as if to peer anxiously at my mother's face, the doctor ceded the space to me, stepping toward the wall that had a faucet on it. There was another nurse in addition to the one I had seen from behind. I was embarrassed about encroaching on a cluster of people with my smelly hair, but thinking it would be odd not to move toward my mother, I approached her head on the pillow, standing as far away from the doctor as possible. With a slight smile, my mother said something to the effect of, "They sucked it out for me," and then, quite clearly voicing her complaint, "I couldn't breathe."

"It's exhausting, coming every day and spending all your time here. When things go on, the health of family members often deteriorates, too, so it's important to rest well at night."

I registered the doctor's concern for me as sarcastic, but his tone was gentle. Then he said, "May I speak with you and your mother for a moment?" posing it in the form of a question although there was no way to refuse.

"I think the pain is now quite intense. In particular, there are several areas in the chest where we're reaching the limit of what we can do. How about you, Mom? Is there anything—that you feel you have to do up until a certain day, or that once you've done this—if I were to ask you plainly, how much longer do you feel willing to keep up this perseverance?"

"I see."

Compared to when I was alone with her in the hospital room, my mother's response gave an impression of cognizance. Moreover, she sounded just like herself when she said those words.

"I don't think I'll be here for long."

"Yes, but exactly how much longer?"

At times, the doctor's tone changes so it sounds as if he's a pediatrician speaking to a child who has a fever. He's a thin man with whiskers on his upper lip—if you ran into him on the street, based on his appearance, you wouldn't think he had much money.

"I'd like to speak to my daughter for a moment. Then there's just one thing I'd like to write down."

"Can you still move your hand?"

My mother raised her hand slightly in response to the doctor's question then quickly lowered it, taking several short breaths. It was clear that the effort was like weight-lifting for her. A strand of hair was clinging to her hand, so I pulled it away. My mother's face was visibly covered in peach fuzz, so I figured that ordinarily, she must have been diligent about shaving it. From the looks of it, my mother had lost about half of the hair she'd had when she was at my apartment. Which was strange, because she was no longer undergoing radiation treatment or taking medication with that side effect. Perhaps her waning will to live extended to her hair follicles.

"You must be tired, but if possible, please take the next few days to think about the things you'd like to do. Whatever that may be, if you need help—whether from your daughter or from us—let us know, and we'll do everything we can."

The doctor took the liberty of including me in the group who would be willing to do whatever possible to help. Within the realm of what I can do, there is probably no action I can take that will save my mother.

"I will," my mother replied and closed her eyes.

The doctor had been staring directly at my mother, but now, still looking in her general direction, he turned his body toward me and then finally his gaze as well, giving me a nod. Thinking he was going out into the hallway, I approached the door, making as if to see him out. The doctor stood in the open doorway, in a spot not visible from the bed, and said to me, From now on, please make sure you're reachable by phone, even late at night—it could be tonight or a week from now. The nurses forced smiles at me, and then they too went out into the hallway. For people like my mother and me, this hospital and this room are clean and spacious—being able to stay here is a luxury. I don't know how long the man who gave me the stacks of bills thought my mother had left to live, but her body must have been worth quite a lot. Her pale figure had been shapely, in a way that really drove men wild.

After the doctor and nurses left, I drew close to my mother, who had opened her eyes. She wasn't looking me in the face, but she was trying to speak to me. Since leaving my place, the only appeals she'd made to me were concrete, such as "I'd like some apple juice" or "My back hurts."

"So, have you quit smoking?"

Somehow my mother had remained alert, and she asked me this in a slightly slurred but still audible voice, to which I answered, I'm going to quit, and the moment I did so, I regretted having come into the hospital without first smoking a cigarette out front. I'd have a smoke before lunch. My mother also used to smoke, at least up until I left the home where I lived with her, and my scars came from her cigarette. Neither my mother nor I would ever forget this.

"Quit now."

My mother's pronunciation was now clearly inflect-ed. Her lips were dry, and I wondered if, once she was asleep, I should put some lip balm on them for her. The peach fuzz on her face didn't seem to bother her, so I figured that was fine. It was bright outside the win-dow. From this hospital, I could see the same sickening, bluish-white sky I'd seen when I went out onto the street from the condo where the host lived.

"You can't know what you don't know."

My mother said this, her voice even more emphatic.

"Huh? What does that mean?"

"Know what you know, that's all."

My mother's words could have been taken as ei-ther her responding to my question or ignoring it—as she closed her eyes again, it seemed as though she was laughing a little. With her eyes still closed, she repeated, "Know what you know, that's all," and then fell silent. An oxygen tube was suspended under her nose. I'd al-ways had the impression that being on your deathbed meant being incapacitated by all kinds of tubes and nee-dles, but my mother, who had known she was going to die for quite some time, was hardly encumbered by anything. Not wanting the conversation to be cut short, I found myself opening my mouth to speak.

"Thanks. I guess. Maybe you didn't hate me so much, did you."

I expressed this interrogative without raising my in-tonation at the end. When I was little, my mother had sometimes ignored me rather than just leaving me or locking me up somewhere. I hadn't liked the poems my mother wrote. With two people in a cramped apartment, one of them a child, it was messy and cluttered with school bags and printed handouts and such. Her poems that ignored the lived experience of such disorder, I didn't find them beautiful. They didn't seem to me like the words a woman who lived in a tatami room and sang in a small club ought to be spinning together. But the world my mother wanted to depict was not a life of tatami rooms, but rather one of herbs she planted in the space that jutted out from the window, exposed to the elements and too small to be called a balcony, and of what stretched out beyond those, in the shadows that fell when evening arrived and obscured the unexceptional cityscape—it was only those very limited things that she seemed to love. The river was visible, only just barely, from the apartment where I lived with my mother. The rule was not to talk to her when my mother was writing her poetry, but I didn't know whether her gazing idly at the river counted as her writing time, so I didn't talk to her then either. I used to think my mother hated not just the greengrocer, but also the neighborhood where we lived and the apartment we lived in.

When I was a teenager, I dreaded being alone with my mother. The burns on my skin, I could show them to my friends to play for their sympathy—especially at first—but once I left home, I didn't show them to anyone for a long time. The first job I got at a bar, I chose that one because my tattoos weren't finished yet, and the staff uniform there for waiting on customers was a suit rather than a skin-revealing dress. At that point I could handle the scars from where she had burned me with the cigarette, but the inexplicably inflamed scars on the back of my arm and my shoulder were unlike anything I'd ever seen on anyone else's skin, and I was ashamed of them. It was tough to leave home at seventeen and scrape by with a body I didn't want people to see. Most of the friends I used to hang out with where I grew up either lived with a guy or lived off a guy's money. If an older girl from the neighborhood who worked in a bar hadn't sublet her apartment to me, I would have been homeless, or else I probably would have ended up back at my mother's place.

I worked in pachinko parlors and izakayas, knowing I wouldn't be able to stay in the older girl's apartment forever, but I kept working in bars—still a virgin—and after I turned twenty, once not just the tattoos over my burn scars but a few other ones as well were finished, I started having sex. But I still dreaded anyone touching the back of my upper arm, especially where it was bumpy and swollen. In my memory, when my mother had pressed the lit cigarette into my arm, she'd had a terribly desperate look on her face, as if she were in a panic and oblivious to anything else. It wasn't her anger that I had felt—it didn't seem like she was angry at me— but she had seemed frantic about something. Sometimes, when I was in the back room at the bar, I'd recall how her face had looked. My mother may have had some idea about what kind of bar I worked at, but ultimately I never told her.

"Soon enough you won't be able to talk."

My mother opened her eyes when I spoke, and she looked at me, saying something like, You're right. Her voice is back to being a little wobbly from the drugs.

"I'm glad I had you."

In my mother's progressively slurring speech, I think I heard what she muttered, but unsure if she meant it as a question, I repeat it back to her just in case.

"I'm glad I had you. I told Papa so too."

It was the first time I'd ever heard her call my dead father that.

The taxi stops in front of the building, and when I get out, my balance unsteady, the sky has already completely shifted from daybreak to morning. The clear and brisk air in what passes for winter indicates that the moon and the month have started over. My leather jacket is short so my ass is cold. I wish I'd worn a scarf.

I go around to the back of the building, push open the heavy door at the rear of the car park, and ascend the interior staircase to the third floor. I would have expected my gait to be heavier but I take each step lightly, my heels making muted clicks on the staircase. At the third floor, I heave my weight against the heavy door that leads to the hallway, and there's a metallic creak. When I came home at night, I would always put the key in the lock and turn it to the left before this door fully closed. However, both my hands are full, making that impossible now. I stand there patiently and deliberately, watching the door slowly close and listening for the sound when it fully shuts. This is the first time I'm aware of hearing it up close. I set down what I'm carrying in one hand, open my handbag to fish out my key, which I now put in the lock for the door to my apartment, turn it to the left, and hear a click as the latch releases. So much that I didn't hear before, when I dwelled in the rhythm between the creak and the turn of the key. Not that there was anything particularly unpleasant in that interval.

I pick back up what I had set on the floor and set it inside the front door. I yank each high heel off my swollen, aching feet, leaving my shoes carelessly in the entryway, and with the strap of my handbag still slung over my shoulder, I head for the bathroom. My face reflected in the mirror looks tired but my skin tone isn't bad. After nearly twenty hours without eating, my body is starving. I wash my hands with soap, dry them on the bath towel I had used the previous morning, and then bring everything I've set down with me as I sit in front of the low table.

I light a cigarette and inhale the smoke, immediately feeling a bit dizzy. I pick up an unopened plastic bottle on the table, twist off the cap, and gulp down some green tea. My lower back is freezing, and that's coupled with a dull, persistent ache.

The day after I stayed over at the host's apartment, I came home from the hospital to find that I had gotten my period. That often happens—I have sex, and my period comes, right on time. On the first and second day, my menstrual flow and cramps are awful, and even on the fourth day—like today—I might still have cramps and lower back pain. I felt like my period had been irregular into my twenties, but after a while I figured out that as long as I had sex even just once a month, my cycle would be almost like clockwork. I hadn't slept with anyone since Eri died, not even customers from the bar, so maybe I'd just had an instantaneous physical reaction to the host's body.

For now, I set down beside me the armful I had been carrying—a paper shopping bag and the two bags of my mother's things—and finish smoking my cigarette. I could just throw out her toothbrush and cup. I'd have to go over to the apartment with a view of the river to clean and clear it out, but I doubted there was much of anything that ought to be kept or needed to be put into the casket. It was not in my mother's nature to needlessly save things. The paper shopping bag holds a small bouquet from the hospital massage therapist who came around to my mother's room a few days prior. I pulled over the bag that, for as long as I could remember, my mother had used to carry around what she needed for work when she'd be away from home for any length of time.

Yesterday my mother, in her hospital room, did not sleep. Since I timed my visits to leave for my apartment when she fell asleep, because she hadn't slept, I hadn't been able to leave. She was no longer speaking at all, her temperature and blood pressure had dropped, and the awful breathing sounds that had been intermittent were now constant. The doctor and nurse would come in from time to time, take her blood pressure and relay numbers that seemed improbable for a living being, say they'd be back, and then leave the room. At some point only the nurse showed up—one time she suctioned out phlegm, but otherwise she just checked on my mother's condition. We were waiting for her to die.

Once when I had squeezed her hand, she had squeezed back a little and looked more directly at me than usual, but with only the short, sporadic sounds of her breathing to go on, I couldn't tell what she might have been trying to say to me. When I let go of her hand, her breathing got even louder, so I held her hand almost the whole time. As the intervals between breaths became increasingly more drawn out, the nurse seemed to hang back by the entrance to the room, on standby. It wasn't as if my mother had anything confidential to whisper to me, so it would have been fine with me for her to come in. One time my mother inhaled loudly, and then stopped breathing. The nurse entered and was about to say something to me when my mother took in another loud breath. That turned out to be her last breath, though because I was distracted by what the nurse was going to say to me, I wasn't looking at my mother's face. I returned my gaze to her, and as I watched, her color and expression undeniably transformed to those of a dead person.

Fighting the urgent need to pee, I listened as the nurse confirmed her death, and while the nurse was wiping her body clean, I went to the toilet in the hallway rather than the one attached to my mother's room. I was in a rush when I went into the bathroom so hadn't checked but after I peed and came out of the stall, I looked in the mirror and my eyes were wide open, like that time I dropped a tab in a club without cutting it in half, just chewed up the whole thing. I hadn't taken any drugs at the hospital and the only thing I'd had before going out was an energy drink. I wondered if my body might have absorbed my mother's narcotics. I looked terrible.

When I got home, the face I'd seen in the mirror was somewhat better. Although my eyes were still sort of unnaturally saucer-like, the hollows of my eye sockets and under my eyes no longer seemed so profound. I figured my mother's bag probably hadn't even been opened during her final stay in the hospital, and knowing that the zipper was stiff, I gave it a hard sideways pull, but except for an initial snag, it opened much more smoothly than I had expected. Inside were notebooks, writing implements, several books, a laptop computer, and an adapter for charging—it seemed like the computer needed to charge for a little while before it could be turned on.

The notebook that first came out of the bag when I unzipped it wasn't so old—judging from the date on the first page, she had started using it after she learned she was dying from this illness. Though occasionally her handwriting was extremely shaky, there were plenty of parts that were entirely legible. Each page of the plain, unlined notebook seemed to have a limited amount of text, mostly just a few lines of notes. Here and there, a few pieces bore titles, which, though they were short, made me think they were some kind of poem. A few seemed like song lyrics. If you told me that my mother had written them, fine, but plenty of them didn't seem like the kind of thing she would have written. A few were accompanied by little sketches, notably a drawing of a cat. Neither my mother nor I had ever had a cat.

As I flipped through the pages, I was a little surprised by the dates. When my mother was at my apartment, dozing on the futon or eating a bite or two of food, she had been so weak that the only thing she could manage by herself was to get up to go to the toilet, but a lot had been written during that time. I can't finish writing my last poem from a hospital bed, she had said, so she had come to my place. But once she got there, I thought she hadn't had the strength or the energy for anything other than basic survival, a stage that had come sooner than I'd expected, and that she had never really intended to write any poems here, that the point had just been to spend a few days with me—I thought it was one or the other, but I didn't know which. It wasn't clear to me whether she'd had the inspiration to write or not, but I had believed that she departed this life without writing that final poem.

As the pages neared the date when I had taken her to the hospital, there was one with a title. A headline with letters in katakana that said, "Door."

—Soon it will be nighttime

—Are you all right?

There was blank space and then the remaining three lines. As I read them, I ran my fingers over the back of my upper arm repeatedly. The unevenness that had always troubled me so, the pads of my fingers couldn't find it—neither the prominence nor the indentation seemed to be there. Even if I imagine a flame, making the barest of sounds as it touches my skin, my arm doesn't ache like it did before.

 —The door will swing shut.

 —When the door closes, no explanation is needed

 —I wish you would close it gently.